PUPPY PALS

Susan Hughes

Illustrated by
Leanne Franson

Scholastic Canada Ltd.
Toronto New York London Auckland Sydney
Mexico City New Delhi Hong Kong Buenos Aires

Scholastic Canada Ltd.
604 King Street West, Toronto, Ontario M5V 1E1, Canada

Scholastic Inc.
557 Broadway, New York, NY 10012, USA

Scholastic Australia Pty Limited
PO Box 579, Gosford, NSW 2250, Australia

Scholastic New Zealand Limited
Private Bag 94407, Botany, Manukau 2163, New Zealand

Scholastic Children's Books
Euston House, 24 Eversholt Street, London NW1 1DB, UK

www.scholastic.ca

Library and Archives Canada Cataloguing in Publication

Hughes, Susan, 1960-
[Novels. Selections]
Puppy pals / Susan Hughes ; illustrated by Leanne Franson.

A collection of four previously published novels.
Bailey's visit -- Riley knows best -- Murphy helps out -- Bijou needs a home.
ISBN 978-1-4431-7025-3 (softcover)

I. Franson, Leanne, illustrator II. Hughes, Susan, 1960- . Bailey's visit. III. Hughes, Susan,
1960- . Riley knows best. IV. Hughes, Susan, 1960- . Murphy helps out. V. Hughes, Susan,
1960- . Bijou needs a home. VI.Title.

PS8565.U42A6 2019   jC813'.54   C2018-906338-6

Photo credits:
Photos ©: cover and backcover dog: feedough/iStockphoto; cover and backcover background: katies_place/Shutterstock; 1: AZP Worldwide/Shutterstock; 1 photo corners: Treenoot/Shutterstock; 93: MPH Photos/Shutterstock; 187: Juniors Bildarchiv GmbH/Alamy Stock Photo; 281: Medvedev Andrey/Shutterstock; 281 photo border: Olia Nikolina/Shutterstock.

6 5 4 3 2 1   Printed in Canada 139   19 20 21 22 23

MIX
Paper from
responsible sources
FSC
www.fsc.org   FSC® C103567

Contents

Bailey's Visit 1

Riley Knows Best 93

Murphy Helps Out 187

Bijou Needs a Home 281

Bailey's Visit

*For my sister-in-law Carolyne Hughes
and her Bella*

Chapter One

Puppies were running across the grass. Dozens of puppies.

Some puppies were black, some were brown, some were white with black spots. One puppy was red and shaggy. Another was grey with a white muzzle. All the puppies had smiling faces and wagging tails.

Kat was sitting on her front steps. Her eyes were closed. She was having her favourite puppy

daydream. And it always ended the same . . .

The puppies jump around, begging for her attention. Her mother and father smile at her.

"Of course you can have a puppy, Katherine," her mom says.

Her dad sweeps out his arm. "Yes, Kat. Pick any one you want!"

Kat smiles, too. She looks at all the puppies, and she tries to choose. The little toffee-coloured Irish terrier that has jumped into her lap? The shy grey schnauzer looking at her, his head cocked to one side? The black pug, so tiny that —

Aidan's running shoe nudged her leg, and Kat opened her eyes. As usual her brother was listening to music. He pulled out one of his ear buds. "Come on, Kat," he said. "Let's go! We're going to be late for school."

Kat sighed. The daydream was over. She sent a mental message to the puppies: *I'll come back and visit soon!*

She ran to catch up with Aidan. The sun was shining. A squirrel chattered at her from the branch of a chestnut tree.

"Do you think Mom and Dad will ever let me get a dog?" Kat asked her brother as they walked.

Aidan shrugged. "You've asked them a million times. They always say no."

"That's because they travel so much for work. But *I* don't!" Kat protested. "And *I'd* be the one looking after the dog."

Aidan bounced his basketball as he walked. "I don't know, Kat. I think you should forget about it for now."

Kat sighed. She knew he would say that. He didn't care if they got a dog. Her parents both liked dogs, but she was the only one who was truly dog crazy.

Kat and Aidan reached school just as the bell rang.

"Later, alligator!" Aidan said to Kat. He hurried over to the grade seven and eight entrance.

"See you soon, baboon!" Kat called after him.

She rushed across the playground. But she didn't get in her lineup. Instead, Kat went over to the other grade four line.

"Maya!" she called. Her best friend hung back as her class made its way into the school.

"There you are, Kat-nip! Late, again!" Maya said, with a grin.

Kat made a funny face at her. Maya had called her "Kat-nip" for as long as she could remember. "You love dogs, but your name is Kat? How goofy!" she'd say. Maya often teased her, and Kat teased her back.

It was all in fun, since they had been best friends forever. Even though they lived at opposite sides of town, they had known each other since nursery school. They played soccer on the same team. They took swimming lessons together.

And, most of all, they talked about dogs together. Maya was probably the only person in the world who loved dogs as much as Kat.

Until this year, Maya and Kat had always been in the same class. But a few children had moved away over the summer. So Maya was put in the grade three-four split class, and Kat was put in the grade four-five split class.

The girls didn't like it. Not one little bit.

School had started last week. The first few days had been tough. Kat hoped it would be better this week, but it didn't seem likely.

"Joke of the day," said Kat. "What does a mother dog call her pups when they come in from playing in the snow?"

Maya thought for a moment. "I don't know. What?"

"I'll tell you at recess!" Kat said, waggling her fingertips at her friend. She turned to run toward her lineup.

"Hey, not fair! Tell me now!" called Maya. "That's torture!"

"Nope! Oh, and I have some really awesome news to tell you," Kat called over her shoulder. "Puppy news!" she added, teasing her friend.

"Seriously? And you won't tell me what it is until recess? You are horrible!" Maya put on her grumpy look, but she couldn't hold it for long. Kat started to laugh, and Maya did, too.

"See you!" Kat called. She ran to the back of her own line, which had just disappeared into the school.

Chapter Two

"So?" Maya asked, running up to Kat at recess. "What does a mother dog call her pups when they come in from playing in the snow?"

Kat grinned. "The answer? Drum roll, please . . . Slush puppies!"

"Agh!" Maya groaned. She had a tennis ball in her hand, and she threw it at Kat. "Take that!"

Kat caught the ball easily and laughed out loud.

She loved telling jokes to Maya. Her friend always responded dramatically, either loving the joke or hating it.

Kat tossed the ball to Maya. They threw it back and forth a few more times.

"Okay, next — the puppy news. What is it?" Maya said.

Kat threw the ball back to her, but her throw was wide. "Oops!"

The ball flew past Maya and onto the field. It landed right in the middle of some boys tossing a football around.

"Uh-oh," Kat said. She went to stand beside Maya.

Then Kat saw Megan and Cora, two girls from her class, pointing at her. They were giggling.

"Nice, Kat," Megan called. "Did you do that on purpose?"

"Do you want to play with your boyfriend?" teased Cora.

"Oh, great," moaned Kat.

"It's your own fault, klutz," said Maya, poking her elbow into Kat's side. "You'd better go get it."

"No way." Kat shook her head. "Not alone."

"Come on. We'll ask your *boyfriend* to give it back to us," said Maya, grabbing Kat's arm and heading toward the field.

"Very funny," said Kat.

She didn't have a boyfriend, and Maya knew it. But one of the boys, Owen, seemed to get all tongue-tied when Kat was around. Sometimes he chased her when the class played tag.

Maya was certain this meant Owen liked Kat.

It seemed like Megan and Cora thought so, too.

But it was Matthew, a boy from Maya's class, who picked up their tennis ball.

As Maya marched Kat toward him, he tossed the ball up and down in his hand.

"Thanks, Matthew," Maya said. "Can you throw it back to us?"

Matthew grinned. He threw it to his buddy Sunjit.

"Sunjit," Kat said. She held out her hands. "Over here. Please?"

"Sure thing," Sunjit said. He tossed the ball to Owen.

Maya and Kat stopped. They both frowned.

"Funny," Maya said.

"So hilarious," Kat added.

Owen blushed.

He froze, looking at them.

Maya nudged Kat. "Basset hound," she whispered.

This was one of the girls' favourite games. They would name a dog breed that a person reminded them of. For example, Kat thought Maya was like an English setter. Elegant. Graceful. Loyal.

Kat looked at Owen.

A basset hound? Yes, she could see it. She began to giggle.

Until Maya softly cooed, "Oh, look at that face. Those lovey-dovey eyes!"

Ugh. No! Kat thought.

"Come on, Owen," yelled Matthew. "Over here. What are you waiting for?"

Owen shrugged and threw the ball to Kat.

"Not back to *them*," Sunjit groaned, smacking his forehead with the palm of his hand.

Maya and Kat laughed and ran back to where they'd been tossing the ball back and forth.

Cora and Megan were still giggling and whispering. Kat tried to ignore them.

"Okay, finally. The puppy news," Maya said. "Spill it. I need to know now!"

And just then, the bell rang.

"Line up, please, students!" called the teacher on yard duty. "No dawdling! To your lines!"

With a moan, Maya grabbed her hair and pulled at it. "I live a life of torment!" she exclaimed.

Kat giggled. Maya would make a great actress!

The girls headed toward the school.

"Okay, okay," Kat said quickly. "Remember I told you my Aunt Jenn was opening a dog-grooming salon?"

"Of course, I remember," Maya replied, rolling her eyes.

The teacher shouted again: "Lines, students! Get in your lines!"

"Well, it's opening today! Aunt Jenn called to let us know last night," said Kat. "My mom and dad are leaving work early, so we can go and see her place after school. And they said you can come with us. If you want."

"That's so cool! We can ask my mom at lunch." Maya looked excited.

The girls took turns going to each other's houses at lunchtime. Today it was Kat's turn to go to Maya's house.

"Miss Reynolds? Do you have somewhere you need to be?" It was the yard duty teacher. She looked at Kat pointedly.

"Right. See you, Maya," Kat said, and off she hurried. She couldn't wait until this afternoon!

Chapter Three

"There it is! Aunt Jenn's place: *Tails Up! Grooming and Boarding*," cried Kat, reading the sign.

She and Maya ran ahead of the rest of the family, past the barber shop, the bank and the hardware store. Then they waited impatiently for everyone to catch up.

Kat's father, Mr. Reynolds, frowned as he came up and read a sign in the store window. "*Walk-ins are welcome*. Don't most dogs walk in?" he asked. "Though, I guess some dogs might have dirty paws, so carrying them in would be better."

"Funny, Dad." Kat grinned. "You know it means that people don't have to make appointments ahead of time. They can just walk in with their dogs."

"Oh, yeah. Right," Mr. Reynolds said, grinning back at her.

But then he frowned for real. "I just hope Jenn can handle it all. Your aunt is a very enthusiastic person — especially when it comes to dogs. I love her dearly. But sometimes she can get a bit carried away with her projects."

"Oh, Robert," said Kat's mother. "You worry too much about your sister! I'm sure she'll be fine. Come on, gang. Let's go in."

"Yeah, let's go," said Kat. She and Maya led the way into Tails Up.

The waiting room had a small couch and three chairs. There was a scale and shelves

lined with bags of dog food. At the front desk was a computer, a cash register and a phone.

There were two customers waiting in the little room. One was a young man who sat with a white Shih Tzu on his lap. The other was a woman with a long-haired Shetland sheepdog, or sheltie, lying at her feet. Both customers looked impatient.

Just then, Aunt Jenn came flying out of a room in the back. She wore a light-blue jacket. Her brown hair was mostly pulled back in a ponytail. A few stray hairs frizzed around her forehead. With her was a thin man holding a tiny chihuahua.

"So, how was she?" the man asked, nervously. "It was Chiquita's first time being groomed."

"She was a natural. Very calm," Aunt Jenn said. "It was a pleasure to groom her."

The man smiled, relieved. He quickly paid his bill and left.

"And, now, hello to you, my loyal family!" Aunt Jenn cried, hurrying toward them with her arms open. She gave each family member a huge hug. "Hello, my Kitty-Kat!" she said. That was her special name for Kat. She lifted Kat right off of her feet!

Then she turned to Maya. "And my most-special niece's most-special friend, you came, too!" And Maya was swept up in a hug, as well.

"The place looks fantastic!" Ms. Reynolds said.

"Yes, well done," Mr. Reynolds added. Aunt Jenn plastered a kiss on his cheek. He patted her on the back awkwardly.

"Oh, it is so nice to have a fan club," Aunt Jenn said, pleased. "Would you all like a tour? This, of course, is the reception area," she said, throwing her arms wide. "When I get a receptionist, this is where she or he will sit."

Mr. Reynolds looked worried. "You haven't hired any help yet?"

Ms. Reynolds poked him. But Aunt Jenn answered cheerfully, "Nope. Can't quite afford it yet."

"Um, excuse me." It was the woman with the sheltie. She was standing now. "I'm Mrs. Fennel, and I have been waiting for quite some time. I believe we are next."

"Oh, Mrs. Fennel," said Aunt Jenn, ruffling Mr. Reynolds's hair. "Don't you think this shaggy guy could use some emergency grooming?" She laughed.

Kat and Maya giggled, too.

Mrs. Fennel frowned. "Oh, well," she said. "No, I meant . . ."

"Your sheltie is beautiful," Kat said quickly. "What's his name?"

Mrs. Fennel's frown vanished. Her face lit up. "Why, thank you. His name is Clarke-Davis."

Clarke-Davis? Kat tried not to giggle again. "I love dogs," she said. "May I pet him?"

"Certainly," the woman replied, pleased.

Kat knelt beside the brown and white dog. Gently she ran her hand over his back. "His hair is so soft," she exclaimed.

"Well, I brush him twice a week. And I have him clipped once a month." The woman turned to Aunt Jenn. "My old groomer moved away last month. I was hoping you might be as good as him, although it's doubtful. No one has ever had a way with Clarke-Davis like Roberto did."

"And what about us?" It was the young man with the Shih Tzu in his lap. His dog was asleep, but he wasn't.

"Mr. Winston, you're welcome to leave Clyde here until I'm ready for him," suggested Aunt Jenn. "I have several kennels in the back room. He'd be quite comfortable there while he waits, and then you won't need to sit here with him."

"Leave Clyde in a kennel?" The man looked horrified. "Never."

"Well, I'll be back in no time," promised Aunt Jenn. "I'm just giving a quick tour."

She pointed to the room that she'd just come out of. "My grooming room."

Kat peeked in. She saw two large grooming tables and two stand dryers. Several grooming brushes, clippers, shavers, shampoo bottles and other equipment were on a table nearby.

Aunt Jenn opened a door to another large room with windows. There were several big kennels in the room. "This is where the dogs waiting to be groomed will stay. If their owners will let them!" She winked at Kat. "And the dogs I board will be lodged here, as well. I guess I could call it the doggy-daycare room."

She pointed to a stairway. "Up there is a big room where I can do some puppy training. And there's a yard out back that I can use, too. So you see? I'm all set!"

"And you're going to live here, too?" Kat's father raised his eyebrows.

"Yup. There's another room upstairs that is now officially my bedroom. And there's a small bathroom and kitchen," said Aunt Jenn.

"Grooming and boarding and training . . . You're planning to do all of these, Jenn?" Mr. Reynolds asked doubtfully.

"Sure am," Aunt Jenn said confidently, with a toss of her ponytail.

Ms. Reynolds gave her husband a look, then turned to his younger sister. "It all looks wonderful," she said firmly.

Aidan pulled out one of his earphones. "Very cool," he agreed, nodding.

"Thanks, Reynolds family!" said Aunt Jenn, with a grin.

As Kat's parents and Aidan went back out to the reception room, Aunt Jenn motioned to Kat and Maya to stay behind. "I don't really want

your dad to know this yet, Kat," she said quietly.
"He'll just think I'm in over my head. But . . .
well, I have a little surprise to show you girls."

Kat and Maya stared at one another. What
could it be?

Chapter Four

"Follow me," said Aunt Jenn. She led the girls to the far side of the room. A kennel sat under the window in the sunshine. But it wasn't empty.

"Oh!" Kat breathed.

"A puppy!" said Maya.

A chocolate-brown puppy lay in a corner of the kennel, all curled up, sleeping peacefully. But he must have heard the girls' voices, because just then he woke up.

He lifted his head and looked at the girls with his beautiful green eyes. Then he jumped to his feet and wagged his tail energetically.

Kat's heart melted.

"His name is Bailey," explained Aunt Jenn. "He's a Labrador retriever pup. He's only eight weeks old. His owner, Kelly, has only had him for a few days, but she found out last night that she has to go out of town for three days. There aren't many kennels nearby, and most of them are large. She didn't want to take him to a big kennel. She saw my sign, so she called just this morning to see if I'd take Bailey until she's back." Aunt Jenn shrugged. "Look at him. I just had to say yes!"

Kat looked at the adorable little puppy. She knew exactly what Aunt Jenn meant. That was one of the things she loved about her aunt: she'd do anything to help a dog.

"I'll just have to scoot out here every once in

a while to check on him," said Aunt Jenn. "And then tonight and tomorrow night, I'll bring him up to my bedroom in a crate. It should be fine." It sounded like Aunt Jenn was trying to convince herself.

"Of course, it'll be fine," Kat said.

She slipped her arm around Aunt Jenn's waist as they headed back to the front door. "Tails Up is amazing, Aunt Jenn," said Kat. "And so are you."

"Totally amazing!" said Maya.

"It's like a dream come true, girls," said Aunt Jenn. "Listen, I'm quite busy today — opening day and all — but I'm sure things will settle down by tomorrow. I'll have lots of free time in the days ahead. So, you're welcome to drop by any time and keep me company. We can chat puppies together."

"Tomorrow, after school? Can we come then?" Kat asked, quickly.

"Please?" Maya added.

"Of course," Aunt Jenn said, with a smile.

The girls grinned at each other. It was a plan!

Chapter Five

The next day, Kat and Maya were at Kat's house for lunch.

"So, how are things in your class?" Kat asked. She dipped a carrot stick in peanut butter and chomped on it.

Maya shrugged. "Not bad. The younger kids are a bit of a pain. And I miss you, of course," she added quickly.

Kat nodded. It was okay. Maya was much

more outgoing than she was. Everyone liked Maya, and she made friends quickly. She was probably already good friends with all the girls in her class. But just good friends. Not *best* friends. Kat knew that spot was reserved for her.

Maya swallowed a sip of milk. "What about you?" she asked.

"Megan and Cora are driving me nuts," said Kat. "They won't stop teasing me. About Owen."

Maya made a face. "He totally likes you, Kat," she said.

Kat rolled her eyes. "No, he doesn't!"

"He's always watching you!" Maya replied.

"Whatever. Anyway, I don't mind when you say stuff like that. You're not trying to be mean. But when Megan and Cora say it, it's different. Irritating. They're trying to get to me. They were like this last year, too. But, somehow, with you there, it wasn't as bad."

"Well, maybe you need to think of a way to get back at them," Maya suggested.

"Get back at them?"

"Yeah. You know. Revenge. Payback," Maya said. "Kat, come on. You don't watch enough bad movies. Don't you know? Revenge can be sweet!"

The girls laughed and finished eating. Then Maya said, "Let's go look at puppies!"

"Yes!" Kat cheered. The girls ran to the family's computer in the living room.

They began admiring photo after photo of adorable puppies. There were Afghans and Dobermans, Wheaten terriers and huskies and more! Each one was ridiculously cute.

"If you could have any puppy, what would you pick?" Kat asked Maya. It was the question they always asked each other. What if someday they were allowed to get dogs? They wanted to be ready to choose! But it was so hard. Each time, they gave a different answer.

"Today, I would choose a Bernese mountain dog," Maya replied. She clicked to a photo of a Bernese mountain puppy. His coat was black, white and rust coloured. He looked as soft as a stuffed animal. "I read that they can be very loving. They're also strong and easy to train. You can even teach them to pull a cart!"

Maya pushed the mouse to Kat. "How about

you?" she asked. "What would you choose?"

"This little guy is my favourite," Kat said, clicking to a standard schnauzer puppy. He had perky ears and a curly black coat, and his eyes sparkled with mischief. "Schnauzers are very smart. They even work as police and guard dogs."

"He's so cute! But, really, how could we ever choose just one?" Maya sighed. "There are hundreds of dog breeds. And mixed dogs are adorable, too!"

"And I always change my mind," Kat said. "Do I want a big dog or a small dog? Do I want a really smart dog, or a really loyal one? I'd love a dog that I could pick up and cuddle up with. But I also want one to run with at the park. They are all so different!"

"We'll just have to adopt a bunch of them!" Maya said, laughing.

That's when Kat got an idea.

"Hey, I know!" she said, grabbing Maya's arm. "Let's make a scrapbook. We can call it our Puppy Collection. It will be kind of like having our own puppies right now. We can make a page or two about the puppies we like the most. We can draw pictures — or print out photos — and put them in the scrapbook."

"That's an awesome idea!" Maya said. "And we can write a description about each one. What the puppy looks like, what it likes to do, what kind of care it needs — things like that!" She was just as excited as Kat.

"We can even name our puppies!" Kat looked nervously at her friend. "Or is that too dumb?"

"No, not dumb. Brilliant again, Einstein!" Maya said with a grin.

"I'll ask my mom tonight if we can buy a scrapbook," Kat said. She couldn't wait!

"I think my mom might have some scrapbook supplies we can use." Maya was practically jumping up and down. "Oh, and I have lots of puppy stickers! Let's print out the pictures of today's puppies to get started."

The girls printed out a few pictures and started daydreaming about puppy names.

"What about Schneider for my schnauzer puppy?" Kat asked.

"Schneider the schnauzer — I love it! It's dignified. It will totally suit his moustache!" Maya said. "What about Bernie for my Bernese mountain dog? Too obvious?"

"It has personality!" Kat replied. "I think it suits him. He looks like he'd be fun to play with."

"Hey, are we still planning to go to your aunt's grooming studio after school?" Maya asked.

"Of course," Kat said. "She said we could. Remember?"

Then she sat up straight. She looked at Maya. Her eyes widened.

"Uh-oh," said Maya. She shook her head. "I know that look," she teased Kat. "Trouble."

"No, not trouble," said Kat. "Maya, I have an idea."

"Exactly! See? Trouble!" said Maya, grinning. "Okay, Einstein. What is it?"

"What if we ask Aunt Jenn if we can help out with Bailey? Maybe she'll let us play with him!"

Maya's eyes lit up. "Maybe she'd even let us feed him. Or walk him!"

Kat clapped her hands together. "Oh, Maya, wouldn't that be great?"

"It sure would," said Maya.

"Aunt Jenn knows how much we love puppies. I'm sure she will let us play with Bailey," repeated Kat. "I just know it!"

Chapter Six

When school ended for the day, Kat and Maya hurried to Tails Up.

"Wow, it's even busier than yesterday!" said Maya.

There were no empty chairs in the reception area. A red-haired woman sat with an Irish setter at her feet. An elderly man had two pugs on his lap. A young couple sat together with a basset hound puppy between them. A well-dressed woman sat alone, putting on lipstick and looking into a small compact mirror.

Kat and Maya were just deciding where to stand and wait when the door to the grooming room opened. Out came Aunt Jenn. She was being led by an exuberant cocker spaniel.

"Oh, Portia. You look just wonderful!" cried the woman with newly red lips. The dog licked

the woman's hand, her tail sweeping from side to side. "I am impressed, Jenn of Tails Up!" the woman said. She looked at her dog from one side and then the other. "I am very impressed. Portia and I will be back in eight weeks. I'll call to make an appointment. Until then." She handed Aunt Jenn some money and followed her eager spaniel out the door.

"Okey-dokey," said Aunt Jenn. She wiped her brow. She smiled when she noticed Kat and Maya.

Aunt Jenn dropped the money into the cash register. Then she waved the girls toward the doggy-daycare room. She turned toward her customers. "Thank you for your patience," she said in her most professional voice. "I'll just be a moment."

As soon as Aunt Jenn closed the door, she punched the air with her fist. "All right! Can you believe it, girls? It's day two, and there are people and dogs lined up to see me! Actual customers with actual dogs! Just like yesterday!"

"This is so great, Aunt Jenn!" Kat high-fived her aunt.

"It's terrific," said Maya.

Aunt Jenn grinned and did a little shimmy with her hips. Then she admitted, "But you know, Kitty-Kat, your dad was right. I'm swamped. I do need to get an assistant of some kind soon. Very soon! We'll have to wait until then to hang out. Okay, girls?"

She glanced at her watch. "I better get my next pooch in here, pronto."

"Okay, Aunt Jenn," Kat said. "But . . . well, how's Bailey? How's he doing?"

"He's fine," said Aunt Jenn. She smiled at the girls. "But maybe we should check on him."

This time, the chocolate Lab was awake. He yipped when he saw the girls approaching. His whole body wiggled as he wagged his tail.

"I've been in to see him several times today," said Aunt Jenn. "He still sleeps quite a bit because he's so young. But I think he might be a bit lonely."

"Oh, hello, Bailey-boy!" said Kat. She poked her fingers through the bars of the kennel, and the puppy licked them enthusiastically.

Then Kat shot a look at Maya. Her friend gave her a nod and a thumbs-up.

Kat took a deep breath. "Aunt Jenn, can we ask you something? Something important?"

"Of course, Kat," Aunt Jenn replied. "What is it?"

"You know how much Maya and I love puppies, right?" Kat began. "Do you think we could play with Bailey for a little while?"

For a moment, Aunt Jenn didn't say anything. She trained her blue eyes on the girls and studied them carefully. "Puppies are very cute," she said. "I couldn't agree more. But looking after them is a big responsibility. Dogs are very precious. And they are most precious to the people who love them best, their owners. When people bring their dogs here, they are putting a huge amount of trust in me. They need to know that they can count on me to keep their puppies safe and healthy."

Kat nodded, but she felt her heart sink.

Then Aunt Jenn went on. "But I do need help here. That's for certain. I'm a little busier than I thought I'd be!" She yanked out her ponytail and made a new, neater one. She straightened her jacket. "And Bailey could probably use a little more attention than I have been able to give him today."

Kat held her breath. Maya was still, waiting.

"So, I'm going to agree to this," she said.

"Oh, Aunt Jenn! Thank you!" cried Kat. She felt Maya squeeze her hand, and she squeezed it back.

"This is to help Bailey, girls," Aunt Jenn reminded them. "You have to remember that he is not a toy. You need to make sure there's nothing he can chew on that will harm him. You must make sure you handle him gently and don't let him fall."

Aunt Jenn opened the door of Bailey's kennel. As she reached for the puppy, he began wiggling even more. He wanted out!

"You have to be very careful to hold him securely." Aunt Jenn showed them how to lift

Bailey out of the kennel. "Puppies are very wiggly and they can easily wiggle right out of your grasp. As soon as you can, hold him against your own body. That will calm him and give you more control of his little, squirmy body."

Aunt Jenn popped Bailey back in the kennel. "Now, Kat, let me see you do it."

Kat felt a rush of happiness run through her. Carefully she opened the kennel door and reached in. She lifted Bailey just as Aunt Jenn had shown her. She cupped one hand under his rear end and his back legs, and she used the other hand to grip his shoulders and front legs. The puppy wriggled with joy, trying to climb up her arms.

Kat quickly pulled him close, hugging him against her chest. Bailey raised his head and licked her chin. Once, twice.

"Very good," said Aunt Jenn. She looked at her watch again. "Maya, your turn."

Kat put Bailey back in the kennel. She was careful not to get his legs or tail caught on the opening. Then Maya practised. She looked overjoyed to be holding the puppy.

"Well done!" said Aunt Jenn. "I think you've both got it. Now, today you can play with Bailey

in this room only. Those are some of his toys." She pointed to a basket. Then she pointed to an area covered with newspaper. "This is where I am house-training Bailey. If you see him peeing or about to pee, please place him on the newspaper. Okay?" She headed to the door.

"Got it," said Maya.

"I'll be back in a bit," said Aunt Jenn. "Remember, don't take him outside. And come and get me if you need anything." Then she rushed back to her customers, and Kat and Maya were alone with the pup.

Chapter Seven

"Hello, little guy," Kat said, softly. She patted the puppy's head. She touched his silky ears. Bailey squirmed and wiggled with delight in Maya's arms.

"Okay, let me put you down, Bailey," Maya said, struggling to hold the excited puppy. She squatted and gently set him on the floor.

Bailey sat on his haunches, smiling up at the girls.

"He's so tiny! Only eight weeks old," said Kat. I've never seen a puppy so young before."

"Me, neither," agreed Maya.

"But look at his paws. They're huge!" Gently Kat lifted one of Bailey's front paws. "That means you're going to be a big dog when you're fully grown," Kat told him.

"Hey, do you think it's true that retrievers have webbed feet?" asked Maya.

"Let's look," said Kat. She and Maya examined the bottom of Bailey's paw closely, spreading it gently.

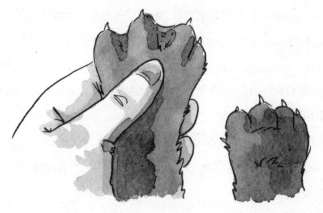

"Hey, it really is webbed!" said Maya. "That is so cool!"

"I read that most breeds of dog have a bit of webbed skin between their toes, though it's not enough to say they have webbed feet. But some breeds, like retrievers, have more webbing," Kat said. "Retrievers were bred to swim out to fishing nets and bring them back to shore. The webbed feet help them swim."

Restless, Bailey licked Kat's fingers. Then he pulled his paw away. He jumped to his feet and looked at the girls, wagging his tail.

"I think he wants to play!" said Maya.

"Good idea, Bailey," said Kat. "Let's do it!"

For almost an hour, the girls ran and tumbled with the puppy. He chased them, and then they chased him.

Around and around they went. Every once in a while, Bailey flopped down on his tummy and rested.

"Bailey has two speeds: full speed and full stop!" Kat told Maya, laughing.

Other times, the roly-poly puppy would go so fast, he'd lose his balance. He'd do a somersault, head over tail.

Finally, it was the girls' turn to catch their breath. Bailey bowed to them with both front paws out in front. It was as if he were saying, "Come on. Just try and get me!"

"We're taking a break, Bailey!" said Kat.

"Yeah, you're wearing us out!" Maya panted.

Bailey turned and sniffed the other empty kennels. Then he found his big basket of toys. With a giant leap, he scrabbled over the side of the basket. He fell right into the jumble of rubber chew toys and cloth tug ropes. He twisted and turned until he was sitting again.

"Bailey, you're so cute!" Kat laughed.

Bailey grabbed a chew toy between his teeth. He shook it hard from side to side, his ears flying in all directions. Then he lost his balance and toppled over onto the toys again.

Maya giggled. "Oh, Kat, I wish I'd brought my camera! We could add Bailey's photo to our Puppy Collection!"

"Next time, for sure," agreed Kat.

"Kat, do you think there will be a next time? Do you think your Aunt Jenn will let us come and play with Bailey again tomorrow?" asked Maya.

"I sure hope so," said Kat. "If she thinks we've done a good job with Bailey today. We need to prove to her that she can trust us, and that we can keep Bailey safe."

Just then Bailey leapt up. His ears flopped here and there as he looked around his basket. He waded through his toys to the side of the basket, attempting to climb over the edge.

Suddenly the whole basket tipped over. Everything tumbled out — all the toys and the puppy, too!

"Bailey!" Kat cried in alarm. But the little chocolate-brown Lab picked himself up. He gave an enormous shake. The girls both crouched down and clapped their hands.

"Good boy, Bailey!" they cried. "Here, boy!"

At once, Bailey's ears perked up and his eyes brightened. He galloped toward the girls at full puppy speed.

"Whoa, Bailey, slow down!" warned Kat. But

Bailey came barrelling toward them. And when he reached the girls, he couldn't stop! He tried, but his little legs went here and there. Bailey skidded into Kat, who fell back on her bum with a thump, knocking over Maya, as well. Girls and puppy lay in a heap on the floor.

Just then the door to the doggy daycare opened.

"Aunt Jenn," cried Kat, her heart sinking. There was her aunt, frowning, her hands on her hips.

Chapter Eight

"Girls?" Aunt Jenn raised an eyebrow.

Kat and Maya jumped to their feet. Kat reached down and scooped up Bailey. "We're fine. Bailey's fine," Kat said, quickly. "We were just playing. Everything's fine."

"Totally fine," Maya added.

Bailey gave a little happy puppy bark. He squirmed and licked Kat's hands. "See?" Kat said. "Bailey's fine."

Aunt Jenn's face cleared. She grinned. "Okay, that's good. I just thought I'd come and say thanks. It's probably time for Bailey to nap again. I'm sure you've tired him out! He'll be fine now until I close up and can spend the evening with him."

Kat nodded, hugging the sweet puppy close to her.

Aunt Jenn wasn't angry.

She wasn't upset.

She could see that Bailey had been safe with them.

Carefully, Kat and Maya put Bailey back in his kennel.

"Bye, my friend," Kat told him, giving him a last rub on the head.

"Have a good little sleep," said Maya. She kissed the palm of her hand, and then she placed the kiss onto the puppy's head.

"Thanks, girls," said Aunt Jenn. "It looks like you did a great job looking after Bailey today."

Kat and Maya held their breath.

They didn't want to ask. They didn't dare hope. But they couldn't say goodbye until they knew.

"So," continued Aunt Jenn, "do you think you two could come again tomorrow. Maybe Thursday afternoon, as well? Bailey's owner won't be back until that night. I'm sure Bailey would like some playmates, especially if I'm as busy tomorrow as I've been so far."

"We'd love to," said Kat. "Right, Maya?"

"You bet," agreed Maya, with a huge smile.

On Wednesday, the girls hurried toward Tails Up right after school.

Kat complained to Maya as they walked.

"Megan and Cora stood behind me in line after recess. Then they started making little kissy noises when we walked back into class," said Kat. "When I turned around, they looked all innocent, and Megan said, 'Oh, Kat, were you looking for Owen?' They are so annoying. Can't they think of anything better to do than bug me?"

Maya shook her head. "I told you. Revenge. An eye for an eye. If they do something mean to you, do something mean back."

Kat shrugged. "Yeah, maybe," she said.

Then all thoughts of school and Megan and Cora vanished — Tails Up was in sight, and there was a lonely little puppy waiting for them!

Once again the reception area was crowded with customers and their dogs. Kat was pleased. Aunt Jenn's business was doing so well!

The girls made a beeline to the doggy-daycare room.

"It's us, your buddies!" Kat called out to Bailey, as they hurried toward his kennel. She saw the puppy jump to his feet and wiggle. He gave excited puppy woofs, asking to come out and play.

"I think Bailey recognizes us!" cried Maya.

Kat lifted up the puppy and gave him the first hug. Then she passed him over to Maya, who covered his head in little kisses.

As soon as Maya set Bailey down, the retriever puppy went off to explore the room again. He sniffed here and there, his tail high. After a while, the girls sat on the floor and rolled Bailey's ball back and forth between them. Bailey raced

after it, excited. The ball was too big for him to hold in his mouth. But he pounced on it like a kitten, and sometimes he managed to trap it between his big puppy paws. The girls laughed while he wrestled with it.

The chocolate-brown puppy had tons of energy, but Kat and Maya were careful to make sure he didn't get into any mischief. He even used his newspaper properly!

Dinnertime came quickly. It was time to put Bailey back in his kennel.

Kat picked him up and snuggled him in her arms, enjoying his puppy smell. The girls stood in the sunshine, looking out the window at the backyard.

The yard was large, and it was surrounded by a chain-link fence. There was a smaller fenced-in area along one side, sort of like a doggy playpen. There were also some bushes and trees for shade.

Kat pointed at a children's wading pool

propped up against the fence. "I bet Aunt Jenn is going to fill that with water for her boarders, one day," she said.

Reluctantly, the girls said goodbye to Bailey. Kat gave the weary puppy a final kiss on the head, and Maya tugged gently on his ears.

"We'll see you again tomorrow, little guy," Maya said.

"Don't worry; we'll be back." Kat put him in his kennel.

"Maybe we should take Bailey outside tomorrow," Maya suggested, as the girls headed home. "I bet he'd love playing on the grass."

"He would," Kat agreed. "And imagine how much fun he'd have splashing around in the pool."

"Well, then, let's do it," Maya said. "Let's take him in the back tomorrow."

Kat shook her head. "Aunt Jenn said we had to stay inside with him, remember?"

"Well, at least let's think about it, okay?" Maya said. "It would be for Bailey, after all. It's his last afternoon with us."

Chapter Nine

All day Thursday, Kat had trouble concentrating on her work. She usually daydreamed about puppies, dozens of them in all sizes and colours. But today there was only one puppy in her thoughts: Bailey.

And the only thing she could picture was how much fun Bailey would have outside. She imagined him rolling in the grass and sniffing at all the outdoor smells. She imagined him free to run full speed from one end of the yard to the other, his ears flying out.

"Kat, are you with us?" asked her teacher.

"Yes, Ms. Mitchell," said Kat, returning to her math problem.

After lunch, it was even worse. The afternoon went so slowly!

When the class was supposed to be working on their stories, Kat found it impossible to keep her mind off Bailey. She couldn't wait to hear his little barks when he saw her and Maya. She couldn't wait to stroke his silky head and tickle his tummy. And the yard? Maybe she would ask Aunt Jenn if she and Maya could take him outside, just for a few minutes.

Kat kept looking at the clock. The more often she looked, the slower the hands seemed to move.

Then Heather, who sat behind her, passed her a note. *Dreaming about Owen?* the note asked.

It had little pink hearts all around it.

Of course, she knew right away who had written it. She looked over at Megan and Cora. The two girls were watching her, their hands over their mouths, giggling.

Angrily, Kat crumpled up the note in her hand.

Then Ms. Mitchell was crouching beside her chair. "Something on your mind today?" she asked Kat, gently.

Kat saw the expressions on Megan's and Cora's faces change. Now they looked scared.

"Yes," she said, nodding. She held the note in the palm of her hand. It would be so easy to show it to Ms. Mitchell. It might finally stop Megan and Cora from teasing her.

"Do you want to tell me about it? Are you missing Maya?" Ms. Mitchell asked.

Kat paused. Maya. It was Maya who had suggested she take revenge on the two girls. Telling Ms. Mitchell about the note would serve them right. They'd probably have to stay in after school. Or they'd have to help out in the kindergarten room at lunchtime. Something.

"Kat?" Ms. Mitchell asked.

Kat wanted to make the girls squirm. But she didn't want to be a tattle-tale. It wasn't like they were bullying her. Not really. And she hadn't even tried telling them to stop.

Kat made up her mind. "My aunt opened her

dog grooming and boarding place in town," she told her teacher. "And I'm helping her by looking after a puppy after school today. His name is Bailey."

"I've seen your aunt's sign. Tails Up, right?" Ms. Mitchell asked.

"That's it!" said Kat, her face lighting up.

"Hmmm . . . That sounds really exciting." Ms. Mitchell knew how much Kat loved puppies. Everyone in the whole school seemed to know! "I have an idea. Since you're supposed to be working on a story now, why don't you write a story about Bailey? That way you can think about him and do your work, all at the same time."

"Okay," said Kat, giving her teacher a smile. "I'll try that."

She picked up her pencil, and right away the words began pouring out. She didn't give Megan and Cora another thought.

Chapter Ten

After school, Kat waited outside for Maya.

When Owen walked past, Kat saw a baseball fall from his pocket.

"Owen, you dropped your ball," Kat said, picking it up for him.

Just then, Megan and Cora walked by. "Kat and Owen, sitting in a tree," Cora chanted.

Megan started to join in.

But Kat had had enough.

"That's it!"
she yelled. The girls
were surprised. They
stopped and looked at her.

"I didn't tell on you in class today. But I still have the note. You need to leave me alone. Owen is *not* my boyfriend," Kat said.

She looked at Owen. His face was completely red. He looked very embarrassed. She hoped she hadn't hurt his feelings.

"But he *is* my friend," Kat added. "And you need to leave him alone, too."

"We were only having fun," Cora said.

"Yeah," said Megan. "You don't have to be so sensitive! Come on, Cora, let's go."

Megan and Cora stomped off across the schoolyard. Kat was shaking. They'd made her so mad!

"I was tired of them bugging me, too," Owen said. "Do you think they'll stop?"

"I think they picked on us because we're quiet. Maybe now that we stood up to them, they'll leave us alone," said Kat. "And, if not, I have proof they've been teasing me. They sent me a note." She smiled and patted her pocket.

"Hi, Kat! Hi Owen!" Maya walked up and beamed at them both.

"Hi, Maya," Owen mumbled, looking at his shoes. "Um, I'd better get going. See you, Kat."

As Owen left, Maya turned to Kat. Her eyes were big.

"What was that about?" she asked.

Kat told her friend about the note Cora and Megan sent her in class. Then she told her how she'd handled it.

"Wow, that's awesome, Kat!" Maya said. "I bet they leave you alone now. You're too fierce to mess with!"

"I hope so. Anyway, we'd better get to Tails Up. Bailey's owner is coming tonight. We don't want to miss our last chance to play with Bailey!"

"Let's go!" said Maya.

Kat and Maya watched Bailey as he investigated an empty crate in the doggy daycare.

He tilted his head to one side, then the other. Then he put his front paws up on the side of the crate and tried to climb on top.

The girls giggled as Bailey

toppled over, then bounded up and tried again.

Suddenly Maya said, "Oh, I brought my camera!" She ran to her backpack and got it out. "We can add Bailey to our Puppy Collection!"

"Good thinking!" said Kat. "Hey, maybe we can add the story I wrote about Bailey, too."

"Yeah!" said Maya. "I can't wait to read it."

Maya started snapping shots of Bailey tackling the crate. Then Kat threw a chew toy for the puppy, and Maya took more photos of him playing with it. When Bailey grew tired of the toy, Kat played chase with him, around and around the room. Maya took even more shots.

Then she paused. "It would be so great if we could take Bailey out in the sunshine," she said. "I know we can't," she added, hurriedly. "But wouldn't it be fun?"

"He'd love it," Kat agreed. "Playing on the grass."

"Smelling the bushes and trees," said Maya.

For a moment neither girl said anything.

"I could ask Aunt Jenn," said Kat.

She looked out the window. It was another beautiful day, but it was getting close to dinnertime.

"I'll be right back," she told Maya.

Kat hurried out of the room and into the reception area. A woman with a shaggy sheepdog was speaking to Aunt Jenn. It was almost impossible to tell the front of the dog from the back!

"Not too short, but I don't want the hair left too long, either," the woman said. "Alice prefers it that way."

As the woman bent down to pat her dog, Aunt Jenn looked over her head at Kat and widened her eyes crazily. Kat couldn't help giggling.

"Okay, I think I have the right idea," Aunt Jenn said, gently trying to hurry her along.

But the woman wasn't done yet. Kat had the

feeling she'd been speaking for quite some time.

"Alice is nine years old," the woman said, "and she is quite particular about her hairstyles."

"I see, I see," Aunt Jenn interrupted, politely. "Well, let's take Alice into the grooming room.

I'll get her settled while you continue with your instructions." She slowly guided the woman and her dog toward the grooming room.

As she went, she shot Kat another kooky look and mouthed, "Help me!"

"She's too busy," Kat told Maya, returning to the doggy-daycare room. "I couldn't talk to her."

"Okay," said Maya. She was holding Bailey. "Well, what do you think we should do?"

The girls went over to the window and looked outside.

"Your aunt told us not to take Bailey outside, but that was two days ago. That was on the first day we played with Bailey," Maya reminded Kat. "She probably wasn't sure yet if we were responsible. She was just trying us out."

"Yeah," Kat agreed.

"I bet if you'd asked her now, she would have said yes," Maya said.

"Yeah, maybe," Kat said.

A squirrel searched for food in the back garden, twitching its tail. What would Bailey do if he saw a squirrel? Kat wondered. It made her smile.

"Hey, what did the tree wear to the pool party?" Kat asked Maya.

Maya grinned. "I don't know. What did the tree wear to the pool party?"

"Swimming trunks," said Kat.

Maya groaned loudly. "Not funny," she said.

The girls watched as the squirrel ran up the side of the fence and jumped onto a tree branch. Bailey's ears pricked up.

"You saw that squirrel, too, didn't you, Bailey?" Maya asked with a laugh.

"The backyard looks pretty safe," Kat said. "There's a fence all around it. I doubt Bailey could get into trouble back there." She patted the puppy's head. "What do you think, Bailey? Do you want to go outside?" The puppy began to squirm and whine. Kat and Maya laughed.

"You do want to go outside, don't you, Bailey?" Kat said. "We thought so!"

"What if we take him outside for only a few minutes? Five minutes. We'll time it," said Maya. She showed Kat her watch. "Should we?"

Kat and Maya stared at each other. Should they do it, even though Aunt Jenn had said not to? She'd placed a lot of trust in them. She'd even let them come back and help again because they'd done such a good job the first day. They'd been responsible and taken very good care of Bailey. Then, again, how could going in the backyard possibly hurt the puppy? It would be so much fun for him. Should they?

Chapter Eleven

Suddenly, at exactly the same moment, both girls made up their minds. They blurted out, "No!"

Then they burst out laughing, because they'd surprised each other — speaking at exactly the same time, saying exactly the same thing.

Just then, Aunt Jenn came flying through the door. She was holding her stomach.

"Aunt Jenn! What happened?" cried Kat. She

placed Bailey in Maya's arms and rushed over to her aunt. "Is everything okay? Why aren't you grooming Alice?" she asked, putting her arm around Aunt Jenn's shoulders.

"Girls, some dog people are so funny! Just so funny!" Aunt Jenn's shoulders were shaking. Kat realized her aunt was laughing!

"Alice's owner decided to book an appointment for a different day. She felt Alice was not in the 'right emotional state of mind' to be clipped today," Aunt Jenn laughed harder. "Especially by a groomer she'd never met." She put her hand to her chest. "Oh, my," she gasped. "Oh, my."

Kat and Maya started to laugh along with her.

Suddenly the girls had the same horrible thought. What if they had taken Bailey outside just now? Aunt Jenn would have seen them! What would she have said? What would she have done? Right away, they knew they'd been right to follow Aunt Jenn's directions.

"You came out to speak to me a few minutes ago, Kat. Was there something you wanted?" Aunt Jenn asked.

Kat blushed. "No, not really, Aunt Jenn." Then she added, in a rush, "Other than, we just wanted to say thanks for letting us help out with Bailey, and we hope his owner is pleased that she boarded him here."

Aunt Jenn came over and patted Bailey's head. He looked up at her with his green eyes and smiled.

"Well, girls, there are two things I wanted to tell you. First, there's good news about the backyard. I have someone coming to fix the holes in the fence. You can't see them from here, but there are several large openings behind those trees. A puppy could wiggle under the fence and be gone in a flash! But once the fence is fixed, we can exercise the dogs out there."

Aunt Jenn had said "we"! Kat swallowed hard but didn't say anything. Maya clutched her arm.

"And the second thing: you've really proven yourselves to me. You've done a fine job following instructions, and you've been so good to Bailey. I hope that you'll be able to help me out on a regular basis. Even if I do get an assistant — I know, I know, I need to do that . . ." She waved her hands around.

"Anyway, I wanted to check with you, to make sure you could still come and give me a hand around here."

Kat and Maya beamed.

"We'd love to!" Maya cried.

"Thanks so much for asking!" said Kat.

"Well, then, it's a deal. Now, I have to get to the next customer. A super cute little pug that needs his nails clipped," Aunt Jenn said. "I'll see you soon, right?"

"Right, Aunt Jenn," Kat said.

As soon as the door closed behind the groomer, Kat and Maya stared at each other.

"Can you imagine if we'd gone outside with this little guy and he'd escaped?" Kat whispered. "You would have found one of those holes, right, Bailey? You're so clever and such an explorer." She reached out and rubbed his tummy.

"You might have got lost. You might have got hurt . . ." Maya said softly. Bailey lifted his head and licked her chin.

"And Aunt Jenn never would have trusted us again! That would have been terrible," said Kat.

For a moment, the girls didn't speak, and then smiles swept across their faces.

"Kat," Maya said. "We get to come and help out at Tails Up all the time!"

"And we'll have lots more puppies to add to our Puppy Collection!" cried Kat.

"Let's play with Bailey a little bit more before we say goodbye to him," said Maya, setting the squirmy little puppy back down on the ground.

He bounded across the floor toward his knotted rope toy. He grabbed it between his teeth and shook it. Then he threw it up in the air. When it dropped, he ran and pounced on it, and shook it between his teeth again.

The girls laughed in delight.

"I'm going to miss this little guy," Maya said.

"Me, too," said Kat. "But we'll add Bailey to our collection, and then we will always remember him!"

Riley Knows Best

For a terrific trio:
Marilena Georgiou,
Alexander Logue and Zackary Logue

Chapter One

Kat was lying on the grass. Puppies were running everywhere! A tiny pug puppy licked her cheek, while an energetic Jack Russell jumped over her chest. Beside her, a young Dalmatian playfully wrestled with a German shepherd.

Kat was surrounded by lovable puppies!

"Kat?" *a voice called.*

Kat's mother joined her on the lawn. "Pick your favourite puppy, Kat!" she said.

But how could Kat possibly pick just one? They were all so sweet. Look, the tiny Shih Tzu could fit in the palm of her hand. The adorable black Labrador was dancing around, begging her to play. The red setter pup was as gangly as a newborn lamb . . .

"Kat-nip!" the voice called again, louder this time.

Kat sighed and opened her eyes. Her daydream was over. She knew she wasn't really allowed to get a dog.

"Hey, lazybones, I'm here!" Her best friend Maya was standing over her. "Come on. Let's get going!"

Kat jumped up. It was time to head to Tails Up, the dog-grooming salon owned by Kat's aunt. Aunt Jenn was so busy, she needed help. She had asked Kat and Maya to give her a hand.

"Coming!" Kat said.

The two girls hurried off toward the salon.

"Sorry I couldn't go to Tails Up right after school today," said Maya. "But there was no way Mom would let me miss my piano lesson. The new puppy will be waiting for us, right?"

"That's what Aunt Jenn said. I wonder what kind of puppy it will be," Kat said.

Her heart felt fluttery. Would it be a low-to-the-ground dachshund? A shaggy sheepdog pup? A ready-for-anything border collie?

"Your aunt didn't tell you?" Maya asked.

"No," said Kat. "When she called this morning, we only talked for a minute. It was kind of an emergency. She asked if we were free to look after another puppy this week. When I said yes, she hung up quickly. She had to call the customer and let her know it could come to board at Tails Up."

Maya grinned. "I'm so excited, I'm bouncing!" she said. And she was!

Maya looked at Kat. "Let's run, okay?"

"Great idea!" agreed Kat.

Kat and Maya took off down the sidewalk. When they came to the main street, they turned the corner and sprinted past several stores and a restaurant.

Panting, the girls came to a stop at Aunt Jenn's

salon: Tails Up! Boarding and Grooming. The bell jingled as they pushed open the door and went inside.

There was no one at the front desk to greet them. Kat's aunt hadn't hired an assistant yet.

She had just opened her business a few weeks ago. She didn't think she'd be so busy. But every day the waiting room was full of people bringing in their dogs for grooming. That's why Aunt Jenn needed Kat and Maya to help out.

Today was just as busy. A young girl was standing next to a West Highland white terrier. A balding man was holding a chihuahua in his lap. Another man was sitting alone, waiting while his dog was groomed. He was snoring gently, his chin on his chest. A big man, he had a pushed-in nose, a jowly neck and a wrinkly face.

"English bulldog," Maya said with a quiet giggle. It was one of their favourite games. When she and Kat saw a new person, they named the dog breed that best matched him or her.

Kat nodded. Perfect.

Just then, Aunt Jenn burst out of the grooming studio. She was wearing her pink grooming apron. Her brown hair was pulled back into a ponytail. "Churchill is all set to go," she chirped. At the end of the leash was a dog with a pushed-in nose, a jowly neck and a wrinkly face.

"An English bulldog! Nice one, Maya," whispered Kat, squeezing her friend's arm.

"Of course, his short coat didn't need to be clipped. But I gave him a good brush," Aunt Jenn explained to the man. "And I gave his face a good wash, especially in his wrinkles on his nose. That needs to be done once a week. I also clipped his nails."

"Thank you," said Churchill's owner gruffly, his cheeks wobbling as he paid.

"Kitty-Kat, Maya!" said Aunt Jenn after he'd left. "Are you ready to meet our newest guest?"

The girls looked at each other. It was time! They couldn't wait to meet the new puppy!

Chapter Two

The girls followed Aunt Jenn into the doggy-daycare room. Four large dog kennels lined one wall of the room. And there, in the last one, stood a beautiful golden retriever puppy. As soon as she saw the girls, she wagged her tail and perked up her ears.

"Say hello to Riley," said Aunt Jenn. "She's a three-month-old golden retriever."

The girls dropped to their knees beside the

kennel. The puppy pushed her nose against the bars. Kat poked her fingers through, and the puppy licked them eagerly.

"Oh, she's so sweet," said Kat.

"She's amazing," breathed Maya.

"Riley's family, the Baxters, brought her home about four weeks ago," said Aunt Jenn. "But the mom and dad didn't know their daughter has a severe allergy to dogs. Ever since Riley came to their home, the little girl has been sneezing and wheezing. She even has hives on her face and chest."

"Oh, no," said Kat. "That sounds horrible." It made her itchy just thinking about it.

"She's allergic to the dog's dander, which is little flakes of its skin," Aunt Jenn explained. Then she winked. "My doggy data for today."

Kat smiled. She hoped that one day she would know as much about dogs as her aunt did.

"So what are they going to do? What's going

to happen to Riley?" asked Kat. She gazed at the plump little pup.

"Well," said Aunt Jenn, "the Baxters know they can't keep her. So they are trying to find her a new home. They think they may have found one, but the new family needs a few more days to decide. Getting a new puppy is a big responsibility."

The girls looked at each other. They knew it, all right. That's why their own parents wouldn't let them get dogs. They said they didn't have enough time to look after puppies.

"The Baxters called me early this morning. They asked if Riley could stay here for a few days until they work everything out. I told them I was busy, but I would check with my helpers." Aunt Jenn smiled at Kat and Maya. "They were thrilled when I called them back and said Riley could come."

"You're the best, Aunt Jenn," said Kat. She

knew her aunt had a soft spot for every dog she met. She could never say no to a puppy in need.

"Now, girls, Riley needs lots of exercise. The holes in the backyard fence have been fixed — only a dog Houdini would be able to get out of there! So you can give Riley a good run-around outside. Oh, and the Baxters were beginning to teach Riley some simple commands. Please practise those with her. There is 'sit,' and this is the hand command." Aunt Jenn dropped her arm and opened her hand, palm out. Then she slowly lifted her hand.

Kat tried it. So did Maya.

"And there's 'lie down,'" Aunt Jenn said, pointing sharply to the ground. "The Baxters were also teaching Riley to come. They call 'come' to her when she's on the leash. That way, they can pull her toward them if she forgets what to do. She gets a treat when she does what they ask."

Aunt Jenn handed them Riley's leash. "So, girls, are you okay with your newest little charge? Do you remember how to take a puppy in and out of a kennel safely?"

"You bet, Aunt Jenn," said Kat, happily. "And don't worry. We'll take good care of her."

"Okay. Heigh-ho, heigh-ho, it's back to work I go!" Aunt Jenn sang. She smoothed down her apron, and off she went.

As her aunt left, Kat carefully opened the kennel door, reached in and scooped up Riley. She stood, pressing the golden retriever pup close to her.

Oh, she felt as soft as she looked! Kat breathed in the lovely puppy smell.

Riley looked up at Kat, her eyes sparkling. Most of her body was a beautiful light-gold colour. Her hair was fluffy, like feathers. She had a little black nose and dark-brown eyes.

"Here you go, Maya," Kat said, setting the puppy carefully into her friend's waiting arms.

"Riley! Nice to meet you, girl," said Maya, gently. She stroked the puppy's soft, golden fur. "You are such a good girl."

Riley licked Maya's hands. The puppy began to wiggle and squirm. She was so happy to have company. And now she wanted to play!

"Okay, Riley," said Kat. "Let's go outside!"

Kat gathered up some chew toys and dog biscuits, and led Maya and Riley out into the sunny backyard. The yard was covered in grass, and there were trees along one side. A chain-link fence went all the way around.

"Here you go, Riley," said Maya, setting her down. For a moment the puppy just sat, looking and listening, her ears turning this way and that. Then she bounded off across the lawn, her tail high.

Riley sniffed the bottom of one tree, investigating all the way around it. Then she raced off to another tree and did the same thing. Suddenly she barked with her paws stretched out in front and her hind end up. She was excited by something in the dirt.

"What is it, girl?" asked Kat.

The girls raced over to look.

"Ants!" cried Maya, laughing. "Black ants!"

Riley barked and barked, wagging her tail, backing away from the insects.

"You are so brave and fierce," Kat teased the puppy.

"Thank you for protecting us," added Maya.

Riley chased a bird and tumbled into a small

flower bed. She scratched an itch on her side with her rear paw and fell over. She found a stick and chewed it. She was so busy!

"Okay, let's play ball!" suggested Kat. She threw a ball across the yard. Riley raced after it and chomped it.

"Now bring it here," called Maya, but Riley wouldn't. She stood watching the girls, wagging her tail. Kat went over to take the ball from her mouth, but Riley thought it was part of the game and raced away. The girls laughed.

"Okay, I have an idea," said Kat. She had another ball with her. She threw it down to the other end of the yard. Riley galloped to it and dropped the ball in her mouth. She picked up the new one. When Kat went and picked up the first ball, Riley didn't mind. She just wagged her tail, waiting for more fun. And when Kat threw it, Riley dropped the second ball and raced to pick up the first one.

"Well, this will work for now!" said Maya. The girls took turns throwing the balls for Riley, over and over again.

Finally, the puppy seemed to tire.

"Time for your lessons," Kat announced. She snapped the leash onto Riley's bright-red collar. She and Maya practised "sit" and "lie down" with Riley. They rewarded her with dog biscuits when she did what she was asked. They also worked on asking her to "come." If she didn't head toward them when they called, they pulled gently on the leash, drawing Riley to them. When she was close, they praised her and petted her.

When Aunt Jenn came to the door to call them in, it seemed far too soon. "Did it go all right?" she asked. "Will we see you tomorrow?"

"We'll be here," Kat said, happily.

Nothing would keep her and Maya away!

Chapter Three

"Come on, Kat!" Aidan called. "You're so slow. We'll be late."

Kat hurried to catch up with her brother.

She was old enough to walk by herself now, but they still walked to school together every day. They didn't really talk much. Aidan was always listening to his music. But Kat didn't mind. Somehow it was just a nice way to start her day.

The bell rang as Kat and Aidan hurried

through the fence that circled Orchard Valley Elementary School.

"Later, alligator!" Aidan said, heading to the grade-eight entrance.

"Bye, bye, horsefly!" Kat replied. She could see her grade four/five class lining up outside the school. But instead of hurrying there, she ran over to Maya's line.

Kat and Maya were both in grade four, but this year Kat was in one split class and Maya was in the other. This was the first year they weren't in the same class. It was hard to get used to.

Still, the girls always tried to say hello before school. And share a joke.

Kat ran up to Maya, who was smiling.

"Joke of the day: What did the tree say to the squirrel?" Kat panted.

Maya thought hard. "That has to be an easy one." Her class line began moving. "Oh, Kat, you never give me enough time," she complained.

"Take as much time as you need! See you at morning recess," Kat teased.

"No way! You always do this. Tell me the answer now!" Maya demanded. But her line was moving away. "Oh, Kat, you're the worst!" Maya turned with a flounce and followed it in. But she lifted her hand, and she gave Kat a quick backward wave to show she was joking.

Kat hurried to catch the tail end of her own line. Even though school had only started a few weeks ago, Kat had a feeling it was going to be a long year. She liked her teacher, Ms. Mitchell, but she really missed having Maya in her class. She was trying to make the best of it, but it wasn't the same without her.

Today, however, there was a surprise for the class.

Ms. Mitchell was standing at the front with a girl beside her. The girl had red hair in long braids. She was wearing a dress with red flowers

on it. Her knees had Band-Aids on them. She wasn't smiling. Her arms were straight down at her sides.

"Please sit down on the carpet, everyone," Ms. Mitchell said.

The teacher bent down and spoke to the girl. The girl just stared straight ahead.

Everyone had already guessed, but Ms. Mitchell said it anyway. "We have a new girl in our class. Her name is Grace."

The girl looked up. She had beautiful soft-brown eyes. But her face was stony. And she stared at everyone, one by one. Kat wouldn't be surprised if the new girl was scared about starting a new school. But she didn't look scared at all. She looked . . . mean.

Megan and Cora were sitting next to Kat, whispering and giggling.

"Say hello to Grace, class," Ms. Mitchell said.

"Hello, Grace," said everyone except Megan and Cora.

Kat said it, too. And, right then, Grace looked at her.

I hope she doesn't think I want to be her friend. The thought popped into Kat's head, and she quickly looked away.

"We're happy to have you with us, Grace," Ms. Mitchell went on, in a friendly voice. "Would you like to tell the class anything about yourself?" She waited, but Grace didn't say anything.

Megan and Cora laughed. Grace frowned.

"Well, maybe later," Ms. Mitchell said with a smile. The teacher began to talk about the plans for the day.

Megan nudged Kat. She had finally stopped giggling. "The new girl. What's her name?" she whispered, pointing at Grace.

Megan never listened. *Ever.*

"It's Grace," Kat answered, annoyed. And, of course, just at that moment, Grace was staring right at them. Great. Now she would know that Kat was talking about her. What if she thought Kat was making fun of her? Just great.

Kat got a bad feeling in her stomach. And then, before Kat could look away, Grace opened her eyes wide. She lifted one lip and made a face at Kat. A really mean face.

Chapter Four

Kat gulped and quickly looked at the floor.

If she were in a new class at a new school, she'd be nervous. She was sure of it. Grace was new, but she didn't look at all nervous. She just looked angry.

"Okay, class," said Ms. Mitchell. "Go to your seats, please. Get out your math workbooks."

Kat went to her desk. Ms. Mitchell followed

her. As Kat sat down, the teacher stood next to her.

"Josh," Ms. Mitchell said to Kat's seatmate. "Would you mind moving to one of the long tables? There's a seat in between William and Angela. I'd like Grace to sit here, next to Kat."

"Sure, Ms. Mitchell," said Josh.

Kat watched unhappily as Josh grabbed his things from inside the desk and hurried away.

"Grace, you'll sit here for now," Ms. Mitchell said.

Grace didn't speak. She just dropped into her seat.

"Here's our math textbook and a workbook," Ms. Mitchell said. She left the books on Grace's desk when she didn't take them.

Kat glanced over at Josh. He was talking happily to William and Angela.

It wasn't fair! Why did Grace have to sit here, beside *her*?

119

"Grace, I'm sure you and Kat will get along," Ms. Mitchell said. "Kat always seems to have a good joke to share!"

Oh, great. Ms. Mitchell had put Grace here because Kat liked to tell jokes. *That's a good reason to never tell a joke again*, Kat thought to herself.

Ms. Mitchell returned to the front of the classroom. She began to explain how to do the math problems written on the board. Kat tried to pay attention. She liked math. But Grace was distracting. The girl put her pencil on one finger, like a teeter-totter, and she used another finger to rock it back and forth. It clicked on her desk each time it hit.

Kat wanted to ask Grace to stop playing with the pencil. But, more than anything, she didn't want to talk to Grace. Grace made her feel uncomfortable. So Kat decided to try to ignore her.

Finally it was recess. Kat and Maya met at their usual spot, under the oak tree by the school gate.

"Okay. Spill. What did the tree say to the squirrel?" Maya said, hands on her hips.

Kat smiled. "Leaf me alone."

Maya smacked her forehead with her hand. "You call that a joke?" she moaned. Then she grinned. "My brother will love that one. Tonight. Dinner table."

Then Maya asked, "So, did you bring the Puppy Collection with you?"

"Right here," Kat said. "Voila!" She presented it just like a magician. She'd been holding it behind her back, hidden in a black bag. She and Maya didn't want anyone

else to see it. They worried the other kids might laugh at them. Like Megan and Cora. Kat knew for sure that they'd tease her. For some reason, they liked to try to embarrass her. Of course, they had been better lately. Ever since Kat had told them to leave her alone.

Kat and Maya sat down and opened their scrapbook. Puppies were the best things in the world. But neither girl was allowed to have one. So they did the next best thing: they collected photos of their favourite puppies or drew pictures of them. They gave each puppy a name and wrote a description about it. It was like having their own collection of puppies. Usually they found the pictures online or in magazines, but they'd also decided to add puppies they met.

Maya turned to the latest page, and a black, curly-haired puppy looked up at them. "Don't you wish we could really meet Lollie?" she said. "She looks so cute! Look at her tiny black nose."

Kat read aloud: "*Lollie is a toy poodle. She has so much energy! You can't hold her back for even a minute. She jumps so high, it's as if her back legs are springs. She is very smart, too.*"

Maya turned to another page. "Here's sweet little Bailey," she said. She was looking at a photo of a chocolate-brown puppy. Bailey had been a guest at Tails Up a few weeks ago, and the girls had helped take care of him.

"It was so much fun playing with Bailey,"

said Kat. "Remember how soft his fur was? Remember how he'd shake his chew toy in his mouth?"

Maya smiled. "Here's what we wrote: *Bailey is a Labrador retriever puppy. He is eight weeks old. He is being house-trained, and he is doing well! Bailey likes to chase toys and shake them. He is very gentle. He likes to give us kisses*."

Then Kat sighed. "Oh, I miss him. But now we have Riley to play with! Won't it be great to see her after school?"

"I can't wait," said Maya. "She's so pretty. Such a beautiful golden colour."

"Hey, did you notice that Riley's ears were darker than the rest of her coat?" Kat asked. "I was reading about golden retrievers last night. They can be any colour from cream to gold. If you look at the ears of a golden retriever pup, you can tell what colour her adult coat will be!"

"Einstein! That is so cool," said Maya. She

looked at Kat admiringly. "You know a lot about different dogs."

"All thanks to the magic of the Internet," Kat said, spreading her hands wide.

The bell rang to end recess, and Kat closed the scrapbook.

"Hey," said Maya. "Our teacher told us that you have a new girl in your class. That's great, right? You're lucky."

Kat lifted her eyebrows. She put the Puppy Collection back into the bag. "Not great. And I can already tell that she isn't very nice."

"Seriously? You can already tell? You just met her."

"Yeah, I can tell," Kat said.

"How?" Maya asked, surprised. "What did she do?"

"Well, nothing really," Kat said. "She just looks mean. And I have to sit beside her." Then she said firmly, "I don't like her."

Suddenly someone moved.

Someone who had been standing on the other side of the oak tree. Someone they hadn't seen there.

Kat turned. That someone was Grace.

Oh, no! Kat's face turned red. She felt terrible. Had Grace heard her?

Kat opened her mouth to speak, but Grace turned and walked away. Kat jumped to her feet. She knew she should follow the new girl. She knew she should speak to her and say she was sorry.

But she didn't move.

"Who was that?" Maya asked. Her large brown eyes were concerned. "What's wrong, Kat?" Then, a moment later, her face cleared. "Oh, that was her, the new girl. Right?"

Kat nodded. "Yeah, it was Grace. Do you think she heard me say I didn't like her? And that she looks mean? She may have seen the Puppy

Collection. What if she tells everyone about it, just to get back at me?"

"Well, we'll just have to hope for the best," Maya said, with a shrug. "Maybe she didn't hear or see anything. Plus, you only just met Grace. You don't really know what she's like yet."

The teacher on yard duty was ringing her hand bell and walking toward the girls.

"Come on, Kat-nip, let's go." Maya gave Kat's hair a gentle pull. "Hey, you can apologize to her when you get back to class. You sit beside her, right?"

"Yeah," Kat said. Although she was really confused. She didn't know what she wanted to do. Grace had started it all by making that mean face. Hadn't she?

Maybe she would apologize. Or maybe she wouldn't.

Chapter Five

As Kat went into her classroom, she had a funny feeling in her stomach. She knew she couldn't talk to Grace about what had happened. Not yet.

Kat sat down without looking at the new girl.

"Time for our library visit," Ms. Mitchell said.

Kat felt better. She'd forgotten that it was library day. Thank goodness! She could avoid Grace for a little while longer.

Kat grabbed her library book from her library bag. Then she rushed to the back of the classroom to line up. When her class went to the library, they had to walk in partners. Grace was still sitting at her desk, and Kat didn't want Ms. Mitchell to force her to be Grace's library partner.

But who would Kat walk with? She had been Heather's buddy last week. But today Heather had already partnered up with Sarah.

Ms. Mitchell was looking at Grace. Then she turned toward the back of the room. Was she looking for Kat? Frantic, Kat turned to the closest person. It was Owen. His best friend, Ari, was away sick today.

Kat stopped to think. Would Megan and Cora tease her if she asked Owen to be her partner? They said he was in love with her, just because he blushed when she talked to him.

Should she do it? Grace still didn't have a partner. Ms. Mitchell was coming toward Kat.

She had no choice. "Owen," she blurted out. "Buddy up?"

Owen blushed. "Okay," he nodded.

Kat stood next to him, uncomfortable. She watched as Ms. Mitchell spoke softly to Megan and Cora. Gently, the teacher encouraged Grace to stand beside the two girls.

Then Ms. Mitchell led the line out of the classroom. Kat didn't want to look, but she couldn't help it. Grace walked along beside Megan and Cora like a gloomy shadow, her face down, her braids dangling.

She'll find a friend eventually, Kat told herself, trying not to feel guilty. *If she can stop looking so scary.*

The class listened as the librarian talked to them about non-fiction books and how to search for them on the shelves. Then they were given ten minutes to think of a subject they were interested in and find books about it.

Picking a subject was easy for Kat. Dogs, of course. And she even knew where to search on the shelves, because she'd done it so many times before. It was especially nice because Megan and Cora were in a completely different aisle of books.

Kat buried her face in her book. She didn't even look to see where Grace was or how she was doing.

But then Owen came over and began looking at books on the shelf right below hers.

"Looking up dogs?" Owen said, without looking at Kat. "I know how much you love them."

"That's right." Kat glanced over at him. She was curious to see what he had picked. "I didn't know you were interested in . . ." Kat peered at the cover of the book he was reading ". . . pigs."

Quickly Owen slammed the book closed and looked at the cover. He blushed. "Oh," he said. "Pigs? Oh, well, not really."

Kat tried not to grin.

Owen shoved the book back on the shelf and grabbed another one. He seemed to begin reading at a random page.

Kat peeked over Owen's shoulder. "Owen, I didn't know you could read upside down," she said.

Owen's face was totally red. "Oh, right. Um, see you," he said and hurried away.

When it was time to return to class, Kat and Owen walked back together. Kat saw Megan and Cora pointing at them. The girls were whispering to each other. They ignored Grace, who trailed behind them. Her face was like a mask.

Lucky for Kat, the rest of the afternoon went quickly, with no shared seat work. She was able to avoid talking to Grace. In fact, she hardly even had to look at her!

When the bell rang at the end of the day, Kat met up with Maya at their usual spot. They hurried to Tails Up and checked in with Aunt Jenn.

"Hello, little Riley!" the girls called, as they burst into the doggy-daycare room. They rushed over to Riley's kennel. The golden retriever puppy jumped up. She wagged her tail and wiggled happily.

"Here we go. Out you come!" said Kat. As she held the puppy in her arms, all her troubles melted away. She bent her head to breathe in Riley's sweet smell. She felt a soft, wet nose press against her chin. Riley's tongue gave her a quick kiss.

"Do you want to hold her?" Kat asked Maya.

"No, just put her down so she can run free," suggested Maya. "She's probably excited to be out of her kennel!"

Kat set her down, and Riley raced straight over to Maya to say hello. Then she ran straight to the back door, sat down and looked back at the girls with her beautiful brown eyes.

Kat and Maya laughed.

"Okay, we understand!" Kat said. "You want out, right?"

The girls grabbed Riley's chew toys and several dog biscuits. When they opened the door, Riley went tumbling out into the backyard. Just like yesterday, she raced across the lawn. She investigated each of the trees, sniffing all the way around. She explored the flower beds. She barked at a squirrel. She grabbed a stick and growled, shaking it in her mouth. The girls laughed again.

"Let's give her some time to burn off some energy before we do her lessons," Kat suggested.

"Good idea," Maya agreed. "Hey, so did you apologize to the new girl this afternoon? Grace, right?" She looked at Kat curiously. "You didn't say anything about her on the way over here."

Kat sighed. She explained that she had chosen Owen as her walking buddy to the library just to avoid Grace. And that even though Megan and Cora had left her alone, Owen had followed her around.

"Well, you did encourage him," Maya teased. "Poor boy. He just wants to be near you."

Kat raised her eyebrows.

"Sorry, Miss Sensitive." Maya grinned. Then she frowned. "But what about Grace? You didn't say sorry to her?"

Kat shook her head and looked away. "No. Not yet," she said.

Kat pointed at Riley and laughed. "Oh, look, Maya!" she cried. "Riley is trying to sniff the flowers!"

The golden retriever pup was in a small garden. She was fascinated by a plant with beautiful yellow blossoms. The plant was taller than her, and the blossoms towered above her. But she was determined to sniff them. She raised her head as high as it would go, but she couldn't reach.

"Riley's up on her back paws! She's balancing!"
Kat said.

Sure enough, Riley balanced for about five
seconds and took one sniff of the blossom.
Then she snapped at it and toppled over into the
flowers.

"Riley!" cried Maya, concerned.

But Riley bounced back up like a rubber ball.
She wagged her tail and came running. Her eyes
were sparkling. Her mouth was full of yellow
petals.

"Oh, Riley. Naughty girl," Kat told the puppy. She tried to make her voice sound stern, but it was hard. Little Riley looked so proud of herself!

"Okay, Riley. Time to do some more training now," said Maya, firmly. "Right, Kat?"

Kat nodded.

"Okay. Riley, sit girl. Sit." Maya raised her hand, palm open, as Aunt Jenn had shown her.

Riley looked up at Maya and wagged her tail. A petal dropped from her mouth. Kat tried to hide a giggle.

"Sit, Riley," Maya repeated. She lifted her palm again.

Another petal fell.

Kat didn't speak. Neither did Maya. Both just looked at the pup and waited.

Suddenly Riley sat. Just like that.

"Good girl, Riley," Maya said, stroking Riley's soft head. "Well done." She gave the puppy a biscuit.

Kat clapped her hands together. "Nice one, Riley!"

For the rest of the afternoon they reviewed "sit," "lie down" and "come" with the pup. Finally Riley lay down and  wouldn't get up. She was exhausted.

"That's all for today," Maya told her. "We have to go now, but we'll be back tomorrow."

Riley wagged her tail happily as Maya picked her up.

Kat sighed as she followed Maya and Riley back inside. When puppies were happy, they wagged their tails. When they were sad or lonely, they whimpered. When it was time for a walk, their eyes lit up.

You could always tell when a puppy was happy or sad or excited. It never tried to hide its true feelings. It never tried to pretend it was something it was not. And it was hard to hurt a puppy's feelings.

But Grace, Grace was different. What was she actually like? Was she mean or not? Why was it so hard to tell? *Why aren't people more like puppies?* Kat wondered.

Chapter Six

The next morning, Kat still hadn't decided whether or not to apologize to Grace. Then she was late, so she didn't even have time to say hello before the class started. Not that she was too sorry about that.

Kat waited to see if she and Grace would have to do shared seat work. Instead, Ms. Mitchell began to teach the class about a kind of poetry called Japanese haiku. She told them that a haiku is a short poem with three lines. The first line has five syllables, the second line has seven syllables and the third line has five syllables.

Ms. Mitchell read the students some examples of haiku. Then she asked them to write their own poem.

Kat looked at Grace out of the corner of her eyes. Grace's chin was tucked down. Her hair fell in front of her face so Kat couldn't see it.

Kat was relieved. She doodled little drawings of puppies across the top of her page as she thought.

A pug puppy. A Nova Scotia duck tolling puppy. A Great Dane puppy.

Then she began to write. It took her a few tries.

PUPPIES
Wiggly, wobbly, soft
Mouth smiling, eyes so trusting
Puppies are the best.

Not bad, Kat thought, nodding her head.

But when she looked up, Grace was staring right at her page. She was reading Kat's poem! Grace's own paper was blank.

I bet she's going to copy my haiku, thought Kat, angrily. And, sure enough, just then Grace bent over her own notebook and began to write.

Grace was a copycat.

Then Kat smiled. She couldn't help it. *A copycat*

copying a poem about puppies! The idea gave her the giggles.

Kat survived until the bell rang for lunchtime. She met up with Maya, and they went to her house to eat.

After lunch, she managed to avoid Grace. But, when Kat came in from afternoon recess, Grace's desk was smack up against hers. Maybe someone had bumped it when they had left for recess. Maybe someone had pushed it too close.

Grace wasn't there yet, so Kat got up and grabbed the edge of her desk. She would just move it back to where it had been. It didn't have to be so close. She gave it a shove.

"Hey!" It was Grace, and she was glaring at Kat. Her arms were straight down at her sides and her fists were clenched.

Kat's stomach tightened. "I was just . . ." she began.

"Yeah, I see. I know," Grace said in a tight voice.

Kat could tell she was trying not to yell.

Just then Ms. Mitchell called, "Okay, class. Attention, please."

Grace sat down and Kat did, too. She kept her eyes on the front of the classroom where Ms. Mitchell was starting her lesson.

But then something caught her attention. She stole a look.

Grace was pulling a folded note out of her desk. Grace's name was on the outside of the piece of paper. She read the note, and then her face went hard, like stone. The note must have said something nasty.

Grace scrunched the paper up into a little ball and jammed it back into her desk. She didn't even look at Kat, but Kat felt a sinking feeling. Grace had seen Kat shove her desk. She knew Kat didn't like her. For sure Grace would think Kat had put the note in her desk.

Kat wondered what it had said. How bad it could have been. Part of her wanted to blurt out that she didn't write the note. That she'd never do anything so mean. But the other part of her was too afraid to talk to Grace. She looked so angry. Kat was afraid of what Grace might say back to her.

Finally the bell rang to end the day. Kat had never been so happy to leave her classroom. It felt like she was escaping something.

Maya was waiting by the oak tree. When she saw Kat's face, she frowned. She put her hands on her hips. In a silly voice, she said, "Listen, girlfriend, I am so over this. You're turning into a total drama queen!"

Kat knew Maya wanted to make her laugh,

so she tried to smile. The girls set out for Tails Up. Kat told Maya about what happened with Grace's desk and the note.

"What did the note say?" Maya asked.

"I don't know," Kat replied. "But it really upset Grace. And I mean *really*."

Kat paused, hoping her friend would say something comforting. She didn't.

"Sorry, Kat. But you're probably right," Maya said. "Grace will think it's you who wrote the note."

Kat nodded, glumly.

"But, hey, what do you care anyway?" said Maya. "You don't like Grace."

"I don't like her, but it's not nice for someone to hurt her feelings on purpose," said Kat. "She may not like me, either, but I don't want her to think I'm mean. I don't want her to think that I'd write a rotten note about her and stick it in her desk!"

"Well, if she knew you at all, she'd know you could never do that," Maya said, as they reached the main street in town. "There isn't a mean bone in your body."

Kat was silent. She wanted to think that was true, but it wasn't. She had plenty of mean bones. For example, when she was little, she had knocked on old Mrs. McCormack's door and then run away. Lots of times, when she'd done something bad, she'd tried to make it look like it was her brother's fault.

"Hey, let's forget about Grace for a while," Maya interrupted Kat's thoughts. "Look, we're almost at Tails Up! We have something much better to do than worry about that new girl, right?"

"You're right," said Kat. She would put Grace out of her mind. They were going to play with Riley! What could be better?

Chapter Seven

About half an hour later, Kat and Maya reached the park. They still couldn't quite believe it. They were there with a real live puppy! Riley trotted along at the end of her leash, excited as ever. She saw a leaf blow past, and she chased it. Then she saw a pine tree, and she stopped to sniff at the trunk.

"Riley is so much fun to watch!" Kat said grinning. "She's interested in everything!"

The girls kept walking, and so did Riley. But instead of walking with the girls, Riley went around the tree. She suddenly reached the end of her leash and had to stop. Puzzled, she looked at Kat and Maya. The girls grinned back at her.

"Now what, Riley?" Maya challenged her.

The perky puppy tried to run to her, but her leash was wrapped around the tree.

"You have to go back around, Riley," Kat told her. "Like this!" Kat ran around the tree, unwrapping the leash as she went. Riley greeted her with wiggles and a wagging tail.

"Good girl, Riley," said Maya. She stroked the puppy's soft fur. Her ears felt like velvet.

The girls and the puppy walked across the grass. There were several rows of trees and bushes along one side of the park. There was a playground at one end. At the other end was a hill with a grove of trees on top. The hilltop was Kat's favourite place in the park. From up there she could see the town on one side and the countryside on the other.

Kat laughed again. Riley was staring in amazement at a squirrel, sitting on a tree branch, chattering angrily at her. The puppy barked at the squirrel and wagged her tail.

"I don't think he wants to be your friend, Riley," said Maya, smiling.

The girls persuaded the playful pup to leave the squirrel. Then Kat cried, "Okay, let's go! Let's run, Riley!"

The girls raced across the grass, and Riley

galloped along with them. When they reached
the other side of the park, Riley flopped down,
exhausted, her tongue hanging out.

"Are your little legs tired, girl?" Kat asked,
with a grin.

But only a few minutes later, the golden
retriever pup had bounced back up. She was
exploring the grass, sniffing here and there.

"Let's run back again," suggested Kat.

"How about you go with Riley. When you turn around, I'll call her. Then you can run back with her," Maya suggested.

Kat poked her in the arm. "You just want to rest!" she said.

Maya did a pretend pout. "Well, really. How insulting." Then she grinned. "Yeah. You're right. So go, okay?"

"Let's run, Riley!" cried Kat. "Come on. Let's go!"

Riley looked up at Kat and smiled. As Kat began running, the puppy leaped excitedly beside her. Kat had to be careful not to get tangled up in the leash!

They ran all the way to the rows of trees and bushes, and then stopped. "Good girl, Riley," Kat said. She reached down and rubbed the pup's head.

But Riley was pulling at the end of the leash. She was looking into the trees and wagging her tail.

"What is it, Riley?" Kat asked. "Do you see something in there?"

Riley was wiggling happily. She continued to pull toward the trees.

"What is it, girl? Another squirrel?" Kat asked, letting herself be led into the bushes. But then she stopped. She saw what Riley had seen.

It was Grace. The girl was sitting there, among the trees. She had a book on her lap, but she wasn't reading. She was staring off into space. And she wasn't smiling.

Chapter Eight

Kat froze. Her mouth dropped open. She felt the bad feeling again. She wished they had stayed at Tails Up. Coming to the park had definitely *not* been a good idea.

Grace looked up and saw Riley and Kat.

"Oh!" she said, getting to her feet. She wore a blue T-shirt and shorts. Now her face was tilted down. "I was just . . . I live near here," she went on. "Right beside the park." She started to sound angry. But Kat hadn't even said anything.

Riley wagged her tail even harder. She pulled at her leash, wanting to go to Grace.

"Is this your dog?" said Grace. She pulled on one of her auburn braids.

Kat didn't answer. She was still surprised at finding Grace.

Riley stopped pulling. Now she sat nicely. She looked up at Grace, waiting to be petted.

Grace didn't come any closer.

"Tell me," she said to Kat. "Is she yours?" Her eyes were fixed on the puppy. Now her hands were bunched up into two fists.

Kat felt an angry red flush travel up her face. This was the girl who had made a really mean face at her. Who had probably copied her poem about puppies. It was because of her that Kat had to be Owen's hall buddy back and forth from the library. And now here she was, getting in the way of Kat's time with Riley.

Grace took a step closer to the puppy. Suddenly her face was scrunching up. She took another step, moving closer to them.

Kat didn't move. She was scared. Grace looked angry again. Why was she making fists? What if Grace hit her? What if she hurt Riley?

Quickly Kat looked over her shoulder. Where was Maya? What should she do?

Riley whimpered. She jumped up and wiggled with her whole body, trying to get to Grace. Kat couldn't believe it. Why on earth was this sweet little puppy being so friendly to the mean girl?

Then Grace said, softly, "I love dogs, especially

puppies." It was almost like she was talking to herself. Her eyes were shining. "Can I pet her?"

Kat wondered what to do.

Grace's face got that mean look on it. Then tears began to trickle out of the corners of her eyes. "Can I? Please?" she asked. Her voice sounded funny.

She was crying! Grace was crying!

"Her name is Riley. Pet her," Kat blurted out. "Go ahead."

But Kat was too late. Just as she spoke, Grace ran past her and across the park.

Riley watched the girl go, her head tilted to one side.

Kat watched her go, too. She opened her mouth to call to her, but no sound came out. She thought about chasing after her, but couldn't decide if she should.

Suddenly Maya was coming through the bushes toward her.

"Where did you and Riley go?" she called as she came close. "I was waiting for you two to run back to me. Were you hiding on me? Trying to teach me a lesson, right?"

Then Maya looked more closely at Kat. "What is it?" She touched Kat's arm. "Did something happen?"

Kat nodded her head. She was confused by what had happened. "Grace . . . Grace was here. She was sitting right there, reading. Riley must have heard her in here, so she dragged me in." Kat spoke slowly, explaining. "Grace asked me if Riley was my puppy and whether she could pet her, and I didn't answer. Maya, she seemed so angry at me. I thought she might hit me. Or hurt Riley."

"Oh, boy," Maya said.

She sat down in the leaves. Kat sank down beside her. Riley immediately jumped into Kat's lap for a snuggle.

"I was scared so I didn't say anything. I couldn't speak or move." Kat rubbed Riley's plump tummy.

"Wow," Maya said softly.

Kat thought for a minute. "But maybe I've been wrong about Grace."

Maya lifted her eyebrows. "What do you mean?"

"Riley was so sweet to Grace. She just wanted to say hello. She wanted Grace to pet her. Maybe Riley is trying to tell me something. Maybe I haven't really given Grace a chance. Maybe she isn't as mean as I think." Kat's voice was quivering.

"Kat, Riley is just a puppy. Puppies love everyone," Maya said.

"Well, maybe," Kat said. "But still. Riley seemed so happy to see her. It was like she wanted to make Grace feel better. There must be a reason for it." Kat buried her face in Riley's fur. "You know, Grace is new. We should feel sorry for her. And she does seem to like dogs."

Maya stared at her. "Seriously? I can't believe you're saying that, Kat," she said. "You're not saying you want to be her friend?" She paused. "You're not saying you want *us* to be her friends."

Kat shrugged. "I don't know," she said, and it was true. She was confused by her feelings.

Kat would do anything for a puppy who needed her help. That was easy. So, why was it so much harder to do something for a person, a new girl in her class?

Chapter Nine

The next morning, Kat still didn't know what to do about Grace. She tried to think about puppies while she waited for her brother. *Puppies here, puppies there. Puppies, puppies, everywhere . . .*

But it didn't work.

Then she tried to think about Riley. *Sweet little Riley, with her beautiful brown eyes, her silky-soft ears and her big, floppy paws . . .*

But that didn't work, either.

All Kat could think about was Grace.

I've got to speak to her, today, Kat decided, as she and Aidan walked to school. Even though just thinking about it made her stomach tight. What would she say? Ask her to be friends? No. Maya didn't want that. She'd made that clear. So what else?

Apologize? Tell her a joke? One or the other would be good.

I'll get it over with and do it right away, Kat thought. *I'll speak to her before school starts.*

But Grace didn't get to class until after the bell rang. Everyone was already at their desks. Grace dropped into her chair as Ms. Mitchell began the morning announcements.

Okay, I'll speak to her at morning recess, Kat said to herself. But when recess came, Ms. Mitchell asked Grace to stay inside for a chat.

Then it was lunchtime. *I'll speak to her now*

for sure, thought Kat. But when the class was dismissed, Kat couldn't find Grace anywhere. Maybe she had gone home for lunch. Or maybe she was sitting alone somewhere, eating. This wasn't easy!

"Have either of you seen Grace?" she asked two girls from her class.

Lindsay and Carly just laughed. "Are you kidding?" Lindsay said. "You're not going to eat lunch with *her*, are you?"

"Good way to lose your appetite," Carly added.

Kat didn't answer.

Instead, she hurried out to find Maya. They were going to Kat's house for lunch.

But when she ran up to Maya, her friend looked down at her feet. "I can't come to your house for lunch today," Maya said.

"Why not?" Kat was surprised. Then, worried, she asked, "Are you feeling okay?"

"Umm . . ." Maya glanced at Kat, and then

looked away again. "No, actually, I'm not feeling great. I think it's better if I go home for lunch." She began to turn away.

"Maya, do you want me to come with you?" Kat asked.

"Uh . . . no. No thanks, Kat," Maya called over her shoulder, and she walked away.

Kat didn't move for a moment. Her feelings were hurt. She didn't believe Maya was feeling sick. But why wouldn't she have lunch with her? It must have something to do with Grace. Was Maya upset about Kat asking Grace to be their friend? Kat hadn't even decided if she was going to do it!

Kat could hardly eat her lunch. She was worried about Grace and Maya. Then she was angry at Grace and Maya. At the beginning of the week, she had had one best friend and no new girl in her class. Now she felt like she'd lost her best friend and the new girl hated her.

It just didn't seem fair!

Kat was a little late getting back to school after lunch, so she missed seeing Maya in the line to go inside. Was Maya really sick? Had she stayed home? Or had she come back to school? Kat didn't know. That made her angry, too.

When she hurried into her own classroom, Ms. Mitchell was asking everyone to sit on the carpet at the front of the class. Kat saw Grace sit right at the outer edge of the carpet. The other students were careful not to sit near her. It was like there was an invisible wall around Grace.

Kat was angry at her. Things had been better before she came here. But Kat also knew that she was the one who hadn't been fair. She had to do something. She got up her courage and she sat on the edge of the carpet, too. Not too close to Grace, but close enough.

"We're going to discuss temperature," Ms. Mitchell said, setting out two glasses of water.

She held up two thermometers. "Could I have two volunteers, please?"

Ms. Mitchell picked Angela and Ari. She gave them each a thermometer to put in a glass.

Then she said, "Before we look at the thermometers, which do you think will be higher, the temperature of the cold water or the warm water?"

That was so easy. Of course the warm water would have a higher temperature than the cold water.

Kat raised her hand to answer. But Ms. Mitchell called out Grace's name, even though Grace didn't have her hand up.

"Grace," said Ms. Mitchell. "Which do you think will have the higher temperature?"

Grace flushed. She opened her mouth to answer. Then she closed it.

It was such an easy question. *Why isn't Grace answering?* Kat wondered. *Didn't she hear the question? Why doesn't she just ask Ms. Mitchell to repeat it?*

Megan snickered. She rolled her eyes, like she thought Grace was stupid.

"Grace?" Ms. Mitchell said again. "What do you think?"

But Grace said, "I don't know." She shrugged like she didn't care.

Now some of the other students giggled, too. Ms. Mitchell said, "Class . . ." in a warning tone.

Kat frowned. Grace must be embarrassed.

But when she looked over at Grace, she couldn't believe it. Grace had that mean look on her face! She didn't look one bit embarrassed. She just looked nasty.

Kat didn't know what to think.

Then suddenly, she remembered what had happened yesterday in the park. Grace had asked if she could pet Riley. When Kat didn't answer, Grace got that mean look. Then she started to cry.

Suddenly Kat understood. The mean look meant Grace was sad and upset. It meant she was trying to stop herself from crying.

That's what she had done yesterday. And that's what she was doing now. She just looked angry and mean, because she didn't want to cry. Maybe she was a nice person, after all. Maybe she was just unhappy about being at a new school.

Kat had planned to apologize to Grace or to tell her a joke. But now she knew she had to do more than that. Even if it made Maya upset.

Chapter Ten

At the end of the afternoon, Kat turned to Grace. She was about to speak but the bell rang. Grace jumped up, grabbed her knapsack and hurried out of the classroom. She must have been waiting to make her escape.

I have to catch her! Kat thought. *I have to talk to her now!*

She ran after Grace. But, to Kat's surprise, Maya was right outside the door, waiting for her.

"Kat, I want to tell you something," Maya blurted out. She looked embarrassed. "I wasn't really sick at lunch. I was just angry. You're my best friend, and I like looking after the puppies with you. And I like doing it alone, with just you."

Kat tried to interrupt, but Maya kept going. She looked sad. "But I was thinking at lunch that you're my best friend because you're so nice. You're kind and thoughtful. And if you think Grace needs a friend," she stopped. "I mean, if you think she needs *two* friends, then that's okay with me."

A big smile spread across Kat's face. "Maya, you're the best. I mean it!" She threw her arms around her friend and hugged her. "I *do* think Grace needs two new friends. I've got to catch up with her and tell her that," Kat said. "Even though I'm nervous!"

"Kat-nip, I've got your back!" Maya grinned. "That's what friends are for."

The girls spotted Grace right away. She was standing near the fence. She kept glancing at the road, as if she were waiting for someone. Her face looked hard as stone.

Kat stopped in front of the new girl and took a deep breath. "Grace, can we talk to you?"

"About what?" Grace replied. She tossed her head, flipping her braids onto her back. "You didn't seem to want to talk to me in the park yesterday."

Kat turned red. "I know," she said. "I want to say I'm sorry."

Grace didn't say anything. She just pulled on the end of her braid.

Kat continued, "Grace, this is my friend Maya. She's in the other grade four class."

"Hi," said Maya, smiling at Grace.

Grace looked at Maya, but didn't say anything. She didn't even smile.

Kat took a deep breath and plunged ahead. "Grace, I just want to say that I know you copied my poem, and it made me angry. But I'm sorry I didn't let you pet Riley yesterday."

"What? I didn't copy your poem," Grace blurted out. Now she looked directly at Kat. She folded her arms. "I can write my own poem. I don't need to copy yours."

Kat considered. She had seen Grace looking at her poem, but she hadn't actually seen what

Grace had written. "No? Okay," she said with a shrug. "My mistake."

"And you're the one to talk anyway, sending me that rotten note." Grace glared at Kat. Her brown eyes flashed.

"Hey, I didn't write that note," Kat said, her hands on her hips. "I don't know who wrote it, but it wasn't me."

For a moment there was silence. The girls looked at each other.

"Okay. I believe you," said Grace.

Kat nodded. "And another thing. I wanted to say sorry for what I said at recess on your first day. Maya and I were talking by the big tree and we didn't know you were there —"

"That's okay," Grace said, quickly. "I didn't hear anything." But her face had turned red. She was pretending she hadn't heard.

Then Grace hoisted her backpack higher on her back. She looked down the street again. It seemed like she was about to walk away.

"Wait, Grace," said Kat. "I want to tell you about Riley. The puppy you saw me with in the park. The one that you wanted to pet."

Grace stopped. "She's sweet," she said.

"She's so sweet," Kat agreed.

"Totally," Maya added.

Grace didn't speak for a moment. Then she said, "You're so lucky to have a dog. I used to have one. Bella. But she died a few months ago."

"Oh, that's terrible," Kat gasped.

"Mom says it's for the best. Bella was a farm dog. We had to move here, to town. Bella wouldn't have liked it," Grace said. "Mom said maybe it was better we didn't have to put her through that big change." She swallowed hard.

"Maybe," Kat agreed. "But still. You must miss her so much."

Grace nodded. "I do." Then her face went hard. Her eyes sort of bunched up.

Grace looked angry, but Kat knew she was trying not to show her real feelings.

She was trying not to cry.

"Riley isn't my puppy," Kat explained. "Or Maya's. Neither of us has our own dog. But my aunt just opened a dog-grooming salon. She's really busy, so she asked Maya and me to help out. We get to exercise any dogs she boards. This week, it's Riley. Her owners can't keep her because their daughter's allergic."

"You are so lucky," Grace said again, softly.

Kat looked at Maya. Should she do it?

She didn't have to.

Just because Ms. Mitchell put Grace in the seat next to hers. Just because Grace was new and unhappy. Just because she had lost her dog. None of those things meant she had to do this.

But Maya was nodding. She even gave Kat a nudge with her elbow.

"Actually, we wanted to ask you something," Maya said.

Grace stared down at the sidewalk. Again she pulled on the end of one of her braids.

Kat started talking. "Grace, I know I haven't been very nice to you. You probably don't like me very much. I don't blame you. But would you like to come with us to play with Riley? We're on our way to see her now. It would be lots of fun."

Grace frowned. "Really? You want me to come with you?"

"Yes." Kat nodded.

"Yes," said Maya.

Grace was quiet for a moment. Slowly her frown disappeared. Her face brightened. "Well, I can't come today. My mom is picking me up and taking me to get my hair cut." She bit her lip. "But maybe I can come tomorrow. I'll ask."

"Well, I hope she says yes," said Kat. "Because, well, you know, when someone's new and you don't know her . . . Sometimes you may think you know right away what someone is like — just by the way she looks or acts — but actually you might be wrong."

Grace looked confused. Kat glanced at Maya for help.

"What Kat means," said Maya, quickly, "is that we want to be your friends."

"Oh," Grace said. And then she smiled. Her whole face lit up.

"But, listen, there's one thing I need to warn you about, new girl," said Maya. She had on her sassy grin. Her eyes twinkled. "It's Kat. She thinks she's a comedian. She can't stop telling really terrible jokes that she thinks are hilarious."

Grace grinned. "Uh-oh," she said, going along with Maya.

"Yeah, uh-oh is right," said Maya, nodding.

"Hey, they aren't all so bad!" complained Kat, also grinning.

"Okay, Kat-nip, prove me wrong. Tell one," challenged Maya.

"Yeah. Go for it," said Grace.

Kat thought for a minute. "How is a puppy like a penny?" she asked.

"I don't know," said Grace.

Maya shrugged. "Me, neither."

"Each has a head and a tail!" Kat shouted. "Get it? A head and a tail?"

"Oh, that is such a bad joke," said Grace, but she was laughing.

"So bad." Maya was shaking her head and clutching her stomach as if she was in pain.

"I know. So bad," agreed Kat, smiling happily.

Chapter Eleven

A short time later, Kat and Maya were playing with Riley in the park.

Just like the day before, the girls stood a big distance apart and took turns calling to Riley and running with her. Riley loved the game. Her ears flew out as she bounded happily across the grass, first with one girl and then the other.

Kat tried to hold the leash out from her body when she ran. She wanted to keep Riley from coming too close to her legs. But all at once Riley zigged and Kat zagged, and both of them fell down in a heap.

Riley took the opportunity to jump on Kat and cover her in wet dog kisses.

Click! Click!

Maya had brought her camera along. "This will be a nice photo for our Puppy Collection. We can label it: *Kat and Dog!*"

"Nice one," Kat said, with a grin.

"We can add it to the drawings we've made of Riley," Maya said. She snapped a few more pictures of Kat, lying on her back. Kat smiled up at her and hugged Riley close.

A best friend, a new friend and a sweet puppy to walk for a few more days! Kat thought to herself. *I am so lucky!*

front right paw ♡

Murphy Helps Out

For sweet Evany Logue

CHAPTER ONE

Puppies were scampering across the grass. There must have been over twenty of them!

Some puppies were brown, some were black, some were brown with white spots. Some puppies had perky ears and some had floppy ears. Some had big, wide paws; some had little dainty paws. All the puppies had sparkling eyes and wagging tails.

Kat was in her classroom, sitting at her desk.

Her eyes were closed. She was having her favourite puppy daydream.

Her mother and father smile at her.

"Of course you can have a puppy, Kat," her mother says.

Her father sweeps out his arm. "Have any one you want!"

Kat smiles, too. She looks at all the puppies, and she tries to choose. The little red Irish setter puppy gazing up at her with the dark brown eyes? The black and white Dalmatian puppy tumbling across the grass? The adorable wheaten terrier pup with the brown face and the black muzzle?

Suddenly the bell rang. School was over for the day, and the dream ended. But that was okay. Kat had puppy plans this afternoon.

"Let's go!" Kat said to Grace, who was at the desk next to hers. The girls jumped out of their seats, grabbed their things and made a beeline for the classroom door. But before they reached it, they heard their teacher's voice.

"Katherine, Grace, where are you off to in such a hurry?" Ms. Mitchell stood at the front of the classroom. She was smiling.

Kat liked her grade four teacher a lot. For one thing, Ms. Mitchell knew how much Kat loved puppies — and her teacher liked puppies, too.

"You won't believe it, Ms. Mitchell!" said Kat. "Remember how I told you my aunt opened up a dog-grooming salon? We get to help her with a puppy today!"

Ms. Mitchell smiled. "How wonderful!"

"Her business is doing really well," explained Kat. "She thought it would take some time to get going, but she was swamped with customers all last week. So she asked Maya and me to help out after school. Did you know that Grace loves puppies, just like me?"

"I had an idea that she might," Ms. Mitchell confessed, her brown eyes sparkling.

Grace chimed in, "When Kat found out, she asked me to help out at Tails Up, too!"

Grace was new to the town of Orchard Valley. She was slim, with brown eyes. Grace often wore her long red hair in braids. She reminded Kat of Anne of Green Gables.

It had taken a few days, but Kat and Grace had become friends. Not best friends, like Kat and Maya — they did almost everything together. Maya liked to tease Kat and make her laugh. She said, "You love puppies, but your name is Kat? That's crazy!" In return, Kat helped Maya with school projects and told her silly jokes. They had been in the same class since kindergarten, but not this year.

But now Kat had a new friend: Grace. And Maya had agreed to try to be friends with Grace too, even though the girls didn't know each other at all, even though they didn't seem to have much in common. Grace was quiet. Maya wasn't. Grace had trouble saying how she felt about things. Maya did not.

Kat was keeping her fingers crossed that her two friends — her best friend and her new friend — would get along. This was the first time they were going to hang out together. They were going to Tails Up together, and Kat had invited both girls to come over for dinner after. Maya had been to Kat's house at least a million times, but it would be Grace's very first time.

"Well, how lovely!" Ms. Mitchell looked pleased. "Any puppy would be very lucky to have you three looking after him. Have fun, girls!"

Kat and Grace hurried out of the school and across the playground. They stopped to look for Maya. They were all walking to Tails Up together.

"Sorry I'm late." Maya ran up, trying to catch her breath. "Okay, let's go. But just tell me one thing: did I miss the answer to the joke?"

"Oh, right, the joke!" Grace said grinning. She rolled her eyes. Every morning, Kat told a joke. Today it was, "Why are Dalmatians not good at hide-and-seek?" As usual, she made her friends wait forever before she told them the answer.

"So tell us, Kat-nip," Maya demanded. "Answer."

"Are you sure?" Kat teased. "You don't want to guess again?"

"Oh, please. Put us out of our misery," Maya said. "Right, Grace?"

"Right!" Grace chimed in.

"Here goes: Dalmatians aren't good at hide-and-seek because they're always *spotted*!" Kat said.

"Agh!" moaned Grace and Maya.

"Worst joke ever!" Maya complained happily, as they all rushed toward Tails Up.

CHAPTER TWO

The waiting room was packed, just as it had been every afternoon since Tails Up opened. Today, a red-haired woman sat with a perky Yorkshire terrier on her lap. Another woman was weighing her schnauzer on the doggy scale. A big man sat with a collie lying at his feet. The dog was panting nervously. Another man, thin and fidgety, sat alone on a chair. He wore black glasses. His long legs were crossed, one foot bouncing.

There was no one behind the front counter. Aunt Jenn hadn't hired a receptionist yet.

The girls stood along the wall, waiting patiently. Grace took a dog magazine from the rack and began reading. Maya elbowed Kat. She jerked her head toward the man sitting alone. "Greyhound. Totally," she whispered. It was one of the girls' favourite games. They saw a person and named the dog breed he or she most resembled.

Kat giggled and nodded. *Yes. A greyhound. Absolutely.*

A few minutes later, Aunt Jenn came out of the grooming room. She wore her pink grooming coat, and her brown hair was pulled back in a ponytail. She cuddled a skinny whippet in her arms.

"Oh, you sweet gal," she cooed to the dog. "Having those toenails clipped wasn't so bad, was it? You don't need to be so nervous next time."

She handed the dog to the skinny man.

Kat and Maya looked at each other and smiled. "Close!" Kat said to her friend. The man's dog wasn't a greyhound, but Maya hadn't been far off.

Grace looked puzzled. "Tell you later," Kat promised.

"Did it go all right? You're sure my Milly is fine?" the man asked, his nose twitching. Clutching Milly in one arm, he pushed at his glasses once, twice. His Adam's apple bobbed in his throat as he swallowed.

"Oh, yes." Aunt Jenn gave the man's arm a reassuring pat. "She calmed right down once I started."

"Yes. Yes. Of course." The man cleared his throat again. "Not sure why she gets so nervous about things. Well, thank you. Goodbye, then."

Aunt Jenn greeted the three girls with a happy smile and waved them into her office. Inside there were two large grooming tables and two stand dryers. Along the walls were tables holding baskets of grooming brushes, clippers, shavers, shampoo bottles and other equipment.

Aunt Jenn closed the door, sank down into her chair and blew out a sigh.

"This is the first time I've sat down all day!" she said. "People have been dropping by with their dogs since I opened my door this morning. And the phone has been ringing off the hook!"

Just then, the phone out in the waiting room began ringing. "Isn't it great?" Aunt Jenn punched her fist in the air.

The girls laughed.

"So, Kitty-Kat," said Aunt Jenn, using her special name for Kat. "I'm relieved that you and your pals can help me out again this week. But are you sure you have enough time? I don't want your parents getting angry with me because you aren't doing your school work!"

"We have lots of time," said Kat firmly. "We can be here every day after school this week. Right, Grace? Maya?"

"Right," Maya agreed.

Grace nodded. She pulled on the end of one of her braids.

"Wonderful. So, let me tell you about this week's puppy." Aunt Jenn popped a piece of gum in her mouth. "Murphy is a three-month-old Shetland sheepdog, or sheltie. Because they are sheepdogs, they have a bit of a herding instinct. That means they like to chase and, well, herd things. They aren't big dogs. They are friendly, loyal and gentle. Murphy's owner, Brad, is away visiting his ill grandmother. He told me that Murphy needs lots of exercise. He likes to run and play." Aunt Jenn lifted her eyebrows. She blew a pink bubble with her gum. "So, what do you think, girls?"

"We'd love to walk him, Aunt Jenn," Kat said excitedly.

"Perfect," said Aunt Jenn, jumping up. "Let me introduce you!" Adjusting her hair into a new, neater ponytail, she led the way back into the waiting room.

The woman with the Yorkshire terrier stood up. "Are we next?" she asked. The Yorkie yipped.

"In a moment, Mrs. Potts and Pixie," said Aunt Jenn with a smile.

Mrs. Potts sat down, grumbling, and Pixie yipped again.

"Are you sure you wouldn't like to leave your dogs with me until I can get to them?" Aunt Jenn asked the two other customers with dogs. "Really, I have a nice big area where they can wait for their appointments."

The man with the collie shook his head. "No thanks. I prefer to wait."

"What about Max?" asked Aunt Jenn. The woman with the schnauzer glanced at her watch and agreed. She promised to return in two hours.

Aunt Jenn asked Maya to take Max's leash. Then they all went into the doggy-daycare room in the back. It was large, with four dog kennels in a row along one wall. There was also a large fenced-in area, like a playpen.

"That's where Max can go," Aunt Jenn said.

Maya led the dog into the pen and unclipped his leash. She stepped back out and closed the gate behind her. Max ran to the water bowl and drank. Then, wagging his tail, he sniffed around the edges of the fence, and finally lay down on the dog bed. In a moment he was asleep.

In the meantime, Kat had spotted Murphy. And Murphy had spotted them!

The girls and Aunt Jenn hurried over to his kennel to say hello.

"What a sweet little guy!" cooed Grace.

"He's adorable," said Kat.

The sheltie pup wagged his tail so hard, his whole body wiggled.

"His coat is such a beautiful colour," said Maya.

"Yes," agreed Aunt Jenn. "And it will stay beautiful even as it changes. Sheltie coats start off light and they darken as the pups grow up."

Murphy was a lovely golden colour, with a

light covering of black on top. He had a white chest and collar. Each of his paws was tipped in white. His nose was black, his tail was black and his eyes were dark brown. His ears were tipped down.

"Murphy! How are you, boy?" asked Kat. "What a sweetheart!"

Murphy wagged and wiggled some more.

"Now, like most shelties, this little guy might be a little shy with you girls. His owner said he takes his time to get to know people," Aunt Jenn said. She opened the door to the kennel. "Here, lift him out, Kat."

Carefully, Kat scooped up the puppy. Murphy squirmed happily in her arms. He poked his nose against Kat's face, then licked her cheek.

He smelled so lovely! Kat stroked his head and then scratched behind his ears.

"Okay, clearly a match made in heaven. Now I must give a brush-and-cut to the very patient

Pixie," Aunt Jenn joked. She blew another pink bubble with her gum. "Girls, I'll see you later."

Once the door was closed, Kat held Murphy for a few more minutes, breathing in his sweet puppy smell. Then, reluctantly, she set him down.

The excited puppy raced over to the fenced-in area where Max slept. Murphy wagged his tail, waiting for Max to wake up and play with him. But Max just yawned and didn't open his eyes.

Murphy wagged his tail again and then began exploring the room, sniffing the bags of dog food, the other kennels and the closed door.

The girls watched, entranced. Then Maya said, "Hey, what about us, Murphy? We want to say hi, too!" She crouched down and put out her hand. "Come here, boy!"

The sheltie pup stopped. He cocked his head inquisitively.

"Come on, boy!" Maya said encouragingly.

Hesitantly, Murphy began trotting toward her. But as he got close, he changed his mind. He veered away, toward Kat, but his paws slipped on the tiled floor. He skidded sideways, then scrambled back onto his feet, ran to Kat and hid between her legs. Once safe, he peered out at Maya and Grace.

Maya burst out laughing and Grace smiled.

"You don't have to be shy of us," Grace said softly. "We're your friends."

Murphy gave his tail one small wag. The girls laughed again.

"I guess he's a little clingy to me because I was the first one of us to pick him up," said Kat.

She bent down and clipped the leash to Murphy's collar. "Okay, tough guy," Kat said with a grin. "Time for the park!"

CHAPTER THREE

The girls left the salon through the back door. Kat was surprised that the puppy was so good on the leash. He didn't wander onto lawns to sniff trees. He didn't lie down in puddles. Instead he seemed to like staying close to Kat. He bounded along beside her, his nose up, his tail high.

Just being with Murphy gave Kat such a feeling of happiness. Looking at the adorable puppy made her smile!

As Kat walked ahead with the pu
listened to Grace and Maya chatting behir

"I read that shelties are protective. They
a lot to warn their family of intruders, u
they're trained not to," Maya said.

"Our farm dog, Bella, was a mutt," Grace s
"We never knew what breeds were in her, l
we thought that there might have been a bit
sheltie. And maybe a dash of husky and a pinc
of hound. We always joked that Bella was like a
secret recipe!"

Maya didn't say anything for a moment. Then
she said, "There are so many great dog breeds. I
keep changing my mind about which one I like
best." She yanked at Kat's hair. "It drives Kat-nip
crazy!"

Kat turned around, and Maya made a funny
face at her.

"I'm not sure what my favourite breed is,"
Grace said. "We never even talked about getting

a dog, or what breed we wanted. Bella just showed up on our farm one day."

"Really?" asked Kat. She wanted to hear more about Bella, but Maya interrupted. "One week, I like pugs best," said Maya. It was like she hadn't even heard what Grace was saying. She went on, "Another week, I like Rottweilers. This week, I would choose a . . . a Lhasa Apso, I think. Do you know what those are?"

Grace began to answer, but Maya didn't give her a chance. "Lhasa Apsos are smallish dogs. They have beautiful long hair that sweeps along the ground when they walk. They have long ears and long bangs. They are like one big hairdo!"

"Bella had long ears," said Grace. "Her hair was a mix of several colours: golden, white, black and brown. What colour are Lhasa Apsos?"

"Lhasa Apsos remind me of a doll I had when I was little," Maya continued. "She had hair that puffed out of the top of her head. You could pull

on it, make it long and then brush it or style it. Once, I even cut my doll's hair!"

That's weird, thought Kat. *Is Maya ignoring Grace? It's like she's having a conversation with herself!*

Maya moved up to walk beside Kat, leaving Grace behind. She linked arms with Kat. "Murphy is doing so well on the leash!" she said. "He's such a cute little guy. It will be so great to add him to our Puppy Collection!"

Kat felt awkward. Grace was being left out. And they hadn't really told her about the Puppy Collection. It was a special scrapbook they were creating. Kat and Maya drew pictures and wrote about each breed of puppy that they liked. They were going to include all the puppies they helped look after at Tails Up, too.

Why had Maya mentioned the scrapbook? Kat wondered miserably. Was she trying to make Grace feel left out on purpose? Grace had probably seen them looking at it at school, but they hadn't really told her about it. Should Kat explain to Grace what the Puppy Collection was, or would Maya be angry?

"Maya," Kat said, in a low voice. "Listen, about the Puppy Collection . . ."

Just then they reached the park. Murphy stuck his nose in the air and sniffed. He began pulling on the leash excitedly. Maya cried out, "Yahoo! Here we are. Let's run!"

"Yes, come on, Grace!" Kat cried, making a point of including her new friend. "Let's go!"

The three girls took off across the wide open field. Kat laughed as the puppy bounded happily alongside her on his dainty paws.

When they reached the playground on the other side, the girls stopped, panting and laughing. Grace bent down and patted the puppy.

"Good boy, Murphy!" said Grace. The puppy looked up at her with his brown eyes and wagged his tail.

"Doggy! Doggy!" A little girl was standing in the sandbox with several other toddlers, looking at Murphy. There were also several children on the slide and the swing set.

The little girl waved her red plastic shovel. She began to run toward them. "Doggy! Doggy!"

Murphy saw her coming and immediately crouched between Kat's legs.

"Want pet doggy! Want pet doggy!" the little girl cried.

Before she could get too close, the little girl's mother caught up to her and scooped her up. "No, honey. We have to ask before we pet a dog," the mother said firmly. "Is it all right?" she asked Kat. "Can my daughter pet your dog?"

"Murphy is nervous of new people," said Kat. "But it's okay to pet him. Just slowly put out your hand," she told the little girl, "and let him sniff it. Then you can stroke him gently."

"Like this," said the mother. She showed her daughter what to do, and then the little girl put out her hand for Murphy to sniff. Murphy was nervous at first. He put his head down low and cowered. But then, as the little girl waited patiently, he lifted his head and smelled her hand. He wagged his tail. But when she reached out to pet him, he pulled back, startled. His whole body was tense.

"It's okay, Murphy," said Kat. "They aren't going to hurt you."

The mother crouched down beside her daughter. She encouraged the little girl to hold out her hand again. Once more, Murphy sniffed the girl's hand. This time, when she slowly reached out to pet his back, Murphy wagged his tail happily.

"Tank you!" said the little girl. She gave a wave as she ran off back to the playground.

"Yes, thank you." The mother smiled and strode after her.

"Why are shelties so afraid of people?" Grace wondered.

"Don't worry. Einstein will tell us." Maya was teasing Kat. "Kat-nip spends hours reading about dogs on the Internet. Her favourite book is *Dog Breeds of the World*. You've read it — what? — about twenty times?"

Kat shrugged. "I know. I'm hopeless," she admitted. Then she explained, "Some dogs are just a little more shy than others. Most shelties

216

start out that way as puppies. They can be upset by noise or strangers. When they are shy or nervous, they might bark or run away. It's important to socialize shelties when they're still young. We need to help this little guy get to know lots of strangers. He'll learn who he can trust and who is safe. He'll be happier!" said Kat.

"I've got an idea," Maya said. "What if we take turns holding Murphy's leash each afternoon? Then he'll get used to all of us. He'll learn to trust people."

"That makes sense," Kat agreed. She turned to Grace. "Here you go, Grace. It's your turn," Kat said.

Then she saw Maya frown.

CHAPTER FOUR

Grace's face lit up as she took the leash. "Okay, come here, Murphy," she said to the sheltie. She took a few steps. "Come with me."

But the puppy wouldn't budge. He stared up at her with sad eyes. He wouldn't move from between Kat's legs.

"Here's a stick. Let's throw it for Murphy to distract him," Maya suggested. "And we can use it to teach him to fetch and to come when we call." She waved the stick, showing it to Murphy. "Here we go! Ready, Murphy? Go get the stick!" She threw it a short distance.

Instantly the puppy sprang forward and ran to the stick. The leash was a retractable one so he could run far and still be safe. Murphy grabbed the stick between his teeth. He growled and wrestled with it. Then he tossed it in the air.

The girls laughed. "Such a fierce puppy!" teased Grace. "Okay, now come, Murphy," she called. "Come to me!"

Murphy looked at her but he stayed where he was, chewing happily on the stick.

"Murphy, come!" Grace called again. "Come here!"

Now Murphy got up. But instead of coming to Grace, he grabbed the stick between his teeth and headed toward Kat. Grace pulled gently on the leash. "Here, Murphy!" she said again firmly. "Come to me, boy!"

When Murphy felt the pull on his collar, he stopped. He sat and looked at Grace. He looked back at Kat, and then at Grace again.

Maya clapped her hands together. "Oh, he is so adorable!"

"Come, Murphy. Good pup, come here!" Grace called, encouragingly. She slapped her hand on her knees.

Murphy looked one more time at Kat but then he headed toward Grace. When he reached the girl, he dropped onto her feet and resumed chewing the stick.

"Good boy, Murphy!" Grace said, patting Murphy's head.

"Way to go, Grace," said Maya, nodding.

Grace threw the stick for Murphy four more times. On the third and fourth try, the puppy came back to her without even glancing at Kat.

Then it was Maya's turn to hold the leash. Murphy was uncertain at first. He looked at Kat, at Grace, and then at Maya. But this time he adapted more quickly. On the second throw, he came straight to Maya when she called. He even wagged his tail when she praised him.

"Time for a break?" Kat asked. She pointed to the edge of the park. There was a hill with grassy slopes and a grove of trees on top. "Want to climb? There's a great view from there."

The hilltop was one of Kat's favourite places in the neighbourhood. She liked to go there on weekends. Sometimes she sat looking out over the park and the town. Sometimes she walked around the woods on the top of the hill to the other side. She sat and looked out over the countryside. Wherever she was on the hilltop, she would dream about having her own puppy one day.

Maya handed the leash to Kat. "Your turn."

"Murphy? What about you, boy? Think you can make it all the way to that hill and up to the top?" Kat asked.

Murphy cocked his head. He wagged his tail. He smiled at Kat.

Kat laughed. "That's another trait of shelties," she pointed out. "I've read about it, and now I've seen it for myself. They really do smile!"

Grace laughed. "Yes, he's smiling!" she agreed.

"Okay, here we go!" Kat cried. "Come on, Murphy!"

The sheltie bounded forward and the girls followed. They ran all the way across the field to the hill. Then up they went, higher and higher.

When they reached the top, the girls flopped down in the shade of the woods. Murphy lay beside Kat, panting. He licked her hand, once, twice. She stroked his round belly.

"I like it up here," said Grace happily.

"Me, too," agreed Maya.

"Grace, I can see your house from here," said Kat. "Maya, that's where Grace lives." She pointed to the street that bordered the park. "Grace, you're so lucky to live right beside the park."

"I wish we'd been able to stay on our farm," said Grace, softly. "But since we couldn't, it is nice to live beside a park. Bella would have liked it."

Grace's family had recently moved to town so

they could be closer to Grace's grandparents. Just before they moved, Grace's dog, Bella, had died.

Kat wanted to hear more about Bella, but Murphy jumped up. He turned toward the trees and barked. His puppy voice didn't sound very fierce, but he barked again and again.

"What's wrong, Murphy?" Kat stood up, holding tightly to Murphy's leash. He pulled hard. He kept barking. "Do you hear someone? Is someone there?"

"I don't see anyone," said Maya casually. She rolled onto her stomach. "I'm sure it's nothing."

"Murphy, calm down," said Kat firmly. She couldn't tell if the puppy was scared or excited. Maybe both.

"What should we do?" Grace had scrambled to her feet. She looked nervously into the woods. Her arms were straight at her sides. Her hands were tight fists. "What if someone's there? Once, when Bella and I were out . . ."

"Seriously, Grace?" Maya said. She laughed. "You're scared just because this sweet little guy is barking? Just calm down."

"First of all, I am calm." Grace frowned at Maya. "Second, sometimes dogs sense things we can't. They know when there's danger."

"Oh, you're the dog expert now, are you?" Maya said.

"No, but I did actually own a dog," Grace said defensively. "Did you?"

Maya glared at Grace. Then she shrugged. "Whatever."

Kat's heart was pounding. Her friends were fighting! Murphy was barking! What was going on?

CHAPTER FIVE

"Well, if this is such a big deal, let's not just sit here," said Maya. "Come on. Let's find out what Murphy is worried about."

"Well, I'm not going in those woods," said Grace firmly. She crossed her arms.

"No kidding. I am so surprised," Maya said dryly. "Kat?"

Kat hesitated. She looked at Maya, and she looked at Grace. She felt caught in the middle.

But when Murphy whined and looked up at her, Kat made up her mind. "We'll be right back, Grace," she said. "We'll be okay."

Kat let Murphy lead the way. She held the leash tightly, and she and Maya followed the puppy into the forest. There wasn't a path. They had to push their way through the tangled bushes and pine branches. It was difficult to walk. It was difficult to see.

But Murphy seemed to know where he was going. He was still pulling, but he had stopped barking. He was wagging his tail.

"What is it, Murphy?" Kat asked him again. "What are we looking for?"

They were almost through the small woods and out the other side.

Suddenly, the sheltie puppy stopped. He lay down, putting his chin on his paws.

"Puppies sometimes do that when they meet an older dog," said Kat. "But . . ."

"Look! Right under that tree!" cried Maya, pointing.

Kat looked at the pile of leaves and there, curled up tightly in a ball, was a tan cocker spaniel. She was whimpering sadly.

"It's a dog! Maybe it's lost," breathed Maya.

"Well done, Murphy! Good boy. You're a hero!" said Kat, giving Murphy a quick pat on the back.

As the girls and Murphy hurried closer, the spaniel heard them. It sat up and faced them, wagging its tail. Its silky coat was long on its legs and body, almost touching the ground.

"Oh, look. It's an elderly dog. Its face is grey,"

said Kat. "You poor thing. How did you get lost?"

The spaniel looked at them with sad brown eyes. Its wide ears drooped.

"It's so sweet! I wonder how long it's been here?" Maya exclaimed.

Slowly the spaniel got to its feet. It trotted stiffly straight up to Murphy and gave the puppy a friendly "thank you" lick on the nose. Murphy wagged his tail, happily.

Maya crouched down. She put out her hand. "Come, come and say hi to me," Maya invited.

The spaniel smelled Maya's hand. Then it leaned against her leg while Maya gently rubbed its neck. "It's a cocker spaniel, right, Kat?"

"I think so," said Kat. "I think it's an American cocker spaniel, not an English cocker spaniel. American cockers are a little smaller. Their skulls are rounder and their muzzles are shorter."

"I wonder who it belongs to?" Maya said. "It's not even wearing a collar! No tags, no address, no phone number." She looked into the cocker spaniel's brown eyes. "What's your name?" she asked. "Where did you come from?"

The elderly dog only wagged its tail.

"If it had come up the hill from the park side, we would have seen it," said Kat. "It must have climbed the hill on this side. Let's go right there, to the edge of the woods. Maybe we'll see someone at the bottom of the hill searching for the poor thing."

"Okay," said Maya. Then she spoke to the dog. "Would you mind if I picked you up?" Cautiously, Maya lifted the spaniel. It snuggled into her chest.

The girls walked the short distance and came out of the woods. There were only three streets at the bottom of the hill. Beyond, the town ended and the countryside began.

Right away, the spaniel gave a little woof. Murphy's ears tilted forward.

From far away came a woman's voice. "Tawny! Tawny! Where are you, Tawny?"

The spaniel gave a happy whine.

There, at the bottom of the hill, was a tall, thin elderly woman leaning on a cane. She wore a black dress, black shoes and a pink hat with an enormous brim. She peered around her, looking here and there.

"Are you Tawny?" Maya asked the dog. "Is that your owner?"

The cocker spaniel wiggled excitedly and yipped again.

"Tawny! Tawny!" the woman called, cupping her hand around her mouth. "Where are you, girl?"

"Should I set her down?" Maya asked Kat.

"Yes, I think so," Kat replied. "The dog seems to know this woman. She must belong to her."

Maya set down the squirming dog. It trotted down the hill, as fast as it could go. "Yip! Yip!" it barked.

"Tawny, is that you?" the woman called. "You naughty girl! You come right here."

A few moments later, Tawny reached the bottom of the hill. She pressed herself against her owner's legs. She yipped again.

The girls waited for the woman to look up to see where Tawny had come from. They waited for the woman to wave a thank you to them.

But she didn't.

Instead she reached into her pocket. Tawny sat down nicely, and the woman gave her a treat.

Still, the woman didn't look up the hill. She bent down and slipped a collar around Tawny's neck. She clipped on a leash. Then she slowly straightened up.

Now, finally, she looked up, right at Kat and Maya. Kat smiled and waved.

But the woman didn't wave. She didn't call out. She and the cocker spaniel headed away across the grass. Only Tawny looked back up the hill and gave a last goodbye wag of her tail.

CHAPTER SIX

Kat frowned. "That wasn't very nice. We found that woman's dog and returned it to her. And she didn't say anything."

"Not even a wave," said Maya.

"Oh well." Kat shrugged it off. "At least Tawny is safe and sound now." She glanced at her watch. "It's almost five thirty. Already time to take Murphy back to Tails Up."

Suddenly Kat remembered Grace, waiting

for them on the other side of the woods. She glanced at Maya.

"Maya, what's going on with you and Grace? I know you don't know her very well, but you said you'd try to be her friend."

Maya shrugged. "I said I'd try, and I have. I didn't say it would work."

"Maya," Kat complained. "How can you say you've tried? You've hardly spent any time with her!"

Maya shrugged again. "No, but sometimes . . . you just know about a person." She gave a little shake. "She just rubs me the wrong way."

Kat didn't know what to say, so the girls made their way back through the woods in silence. When they reached the other side, Kat stopped short. She looked around. She couldn't see Grace anywhere.

"Where is she? Where's Grace?" she asked. She shot Maya an angry look.

But just then Grace stood up. "I'm right here," she called out. She'd been sitting under a tree, waiting. "So what happened?"

Kat was relieved that Grace was still there and was being friendly.

She explained about Tawny as the three girls headed back to Tails Up with Murphy. It was awkward. Maya didn't say a word to Grace the whole way. Grace didn't say a word to Maya.

"Goodbye, sweet little Murphy. And thanks again for helping us find the lost cocker spaniel!" Kat told the sheltie pup. She put him in his kennel and promised him that they'd be back tomorrow.

The girls walked together to Kat's house, which was just up the street from Tails Up. But before they went in, Grace took Kat aside. "Are you sure you still want me to come for dinner?" she asked.

"Of course. Why wouldn't I?" replied Kat. She wasn't sure what to do. So she pretended everything was okay, even though she knew Grace was feeling awkward with Maya.

"Hi, Katherine!" said Kat's mother when she heard the girls come in. She came hurrying out her home office. "Hi, Maya! And you must be Grace. It's very nice to meet you." She smiled at Kat's new friend. "I'm glad you're having dinner with us tonight!"

"Thanks. Me, too," said Grace shyly.

"We'll be up in my room, Mom," said Kat. "You'll call us when it's time to set the table?"

"Count on it!"

The girls went up to Kat's bedroom. When Grace stepped inside, she caught her breath. The walls were covered in posters and pictures of puppies. The shelves of the bookcase were filled

with books about puppies and even stuffed toy puppies.

Maya flopped down on the bed with her back to Grace. "Can you tell this girl is a *tiny* bit dog crazy?"

"What a great room!" Grace said. "I love it!" Then she made a face. "Oh, my mom told me to call when we got here. Can you show me where the phone is, Kat?"

"Sure. It's in our den." Kat took Grace down the hall and into the den and then returned to her room. She sat down and stared at Maya. "Listen, Maya," she said, "when we started our walk with Murphy, you mentioned the Puppy Collection. In front of Grace. But she doesn't really know about it yet."

"So?" Maya said. She rolled over onto her back. She plumped Kat's pillow under her head.

Kat hesitated. Maya wasn't making this easy. "So, I want to tell her about it. I want her to help us with it."

Maya didn't say anything.

"What do you think? She loves puppies, too. If she's going to be our friend, we should ask her to help us with our Puppy Collection," said Kat. There. She'd said it. She held her breath.

Maya frowned.

"Remember when you first met Grace? You didn't like her right away. Now, apparently, you do. Well, it's a lot to expect that I'll like her right away, too. Besides, just because I said I'd try to be her friend, doesn't mean she has to do everything with us." Maya sat up on the bed. "You asked me to help you at Tails Up. Then you asked her. Fine. You and I came up with the idea for the Puppy Collection. And now you want her to help with it, too." Maya crossed her arms. "Well, maybe I don't want her to know about it."

The girls stared at each other in silence.

Grace came back into the room. Her face was stony. Her fists were clenched. She didn't look at Kat or Maya. "I have to go," she said in a low voice.

Kat jumped up. Oh no. Grace must have heard them talking. "But . . ."

"My mom changed her mind," Grace continued. "She wants me home for dinner."

Kat was sure they had hurt her feelings. "Grace . . ."

"I'm sorry, Kat," Grace said. Her eyes slid to Kat's and then away. "Maybe I can come another day."

"Grace, is that really true?" asked Kat. "Did your mom—"

Maya interrupted. "That's too bad," she told Grace. "See you tomorrow at school."

"Yeah. See you," Grace replied. "Bye, Kat," she added, and she left the bedroom, closing the door behind her.

CHAPTER SEVEN

Kat glared at Maya. "That was not very nice," she said. "Grace is my friend."

"Oh, is she? Well, I thought I was your friend," Maya replied. She was still sitting on Kat's bed.

Kat blinked. "You know you're my friend. But Grace is, too. And it wasn't very nice for you to . . . dismiss her like that."

Kat went to the bedroom door. "I'm going to go and say a real goodbye," she told Maya.

But as she left her room, she heard the front door close. Kat pounded down the stairs.

"I'll be right back, Mom," she called. She hurried out onto her front porch. Grace was running. She was halfway down the street.

"Grace! Wait!" she cried. But Grace must not have heard, because she kept running.

By the time Kat caught up to her friend, the girls were close to the park, more than half-way to Grace's house. Not only had Grace stopped running, but she'd even stopped walking.

"Grace! I'm sorry," Kat told her, trying to catch her breath.

Grace held up her hand. "Shhh . . . Listen."

The girls stood together, quiet.

Then, there it was — the sound of a dog whimpering.

"I hear it!" Kat said. "But where's it coming from? Where's the dog?"

"Over here, I think," Grace said.

Kat followed her across the street and into the park.

"Yip! Yip!" A cocker spaniel was walking slowly across the field. As the girls watched, she sat down to rest. She looked sad.

"I don't believe it. It's Tawny!" cried Maya.

Kat and Grace turned around in surprise. Maya was right there behind them.

Maya shrugged. "Well, I wasn't going to stay at your place all by myself," she said to Kat.

Kat frowned, but she turned her attention back to the cocker spaniel and Grace.

"This is the lost dog, Tawny," Kat told Grace. "The one Murphy found on the hill."

"Tawny, come here, girl," called Maya, gently. "What are you doing here?" She crouched down and patted the dog's head. "Where's your owner this time?"

Kat looked up and down the street. There was no tall woman in a black dress anywhere in sight.

Maya scooped the dog up into her arms.

Grace came to stand next to Maya. "Oh, she's so sad." Grace's voice was trembling. "Can I pet her?"

Maya didn't look at Grace. "Sure," she said.

"But what's happened? Why does she keep getting loose?" Kat said.

"At least she has her collar on this time," Maya pointed out.

Grace bent closer to Tawny, examining the cocker spaniel's collar. "Oh no. Looks like her tags have fallen off! She doesn't even have a registration tag on her collar, so we don't have any way of finding out where she lives." Grace frowned. "Her owner doesn't seem very responsible."

Maya shook her head. "No, she doesn't."

"Well, luckily we have an idea of where Tawny lives. Probably near the bottom of the hill where Tawny's owner stood calling her, right?" Kat suggested. "We should try to take her back there. We might be able to find the right house."

"I don't know about that." Grace put her hands on her hips. "Maybe this woman doesn't deserve to have a dog. She's lost her dog twice? That's terrible."

"You know, I actually agree with Grace," Maya said firmly. "Losing your dog twice in one day? Pretty sad."

"Having a dog is a privilege," said Grace. "I'd give anything to have my own dog back. And here's someone with a dog and she doesn't care that it's gone . . ."

"Yeah, we don't even know if we can find her.

Maybe we shouldn't try," said Maya.

Grace nodded. "Yeah."

Kat was confused. Maya had treated Grace badly all day, so she was happy the two girls were finally agreeing on something. But not even try to find Tawny's owner? Kat wasn't sure she could agree with Maya and Grace on that.

Kat's thoughts tumbled and turned. If they didn't try to find the owner, maybe the three of them could keep Tawny. They could take turns. How could her parents say no to her looking after a lost dog?

Maybe. Or was Kat just being selfish?

It was exciting to think about having a dog. It was what Kat had always wanted. But when she thought about keeping Tawny, she felt excited and sad at the same time. It was like the feelings were wrestling inside her.

Kat reached down and petted Tawny. The little elderly cocker spaniel was now sitting, resting her legs. She looked like she was counting on the girls to do what was right.

Suddenly Kat knew. She'd been thinking of it all wrong. They had to put Tawny's needs first.

"Listen," she said. "We don't know anything about Tawny's owner. Tawny is lost, and she's sad. She needs to go home."

"But just because Tawny is sad, it doesn't mean her owner is taking good care of her," said Maya. "Maybe she's just really loyal."

"Some dogs put up with a lot from their owners and still love them," Grace pointed out.

"So, we'll try to find Tawny's home, and we'll do our best to check out her owner. We won't leave her there if we think she isn't safe," said Kat. "Agreed?"

Grace hesitated. She frowned as she considered Kat's suggestion. Then she nodded. "Agreed," she said.

"Yes, agreed. Okay, Kat," Maya said

impatiently. Then she gave a dramatic sigh. "Kat-nip is almost always right," Maya told Grace. "You'll have to get used to it. It's just one of the hardships of being her friend."

Grace grinned. "I'll try," she said.

Kat rolled her eyes, but she was relieved that the two girls were finally getting along.

"Okay, so we'll head over with Tawny to her neighbourhood? Scout out the area?" Maya asked. As usual, with the decision made, Maya wanted to leap into action.

"Okay. But it might take a while," said Kat. "Tawny seems pretty lost."

"Hey, I know!" Grace's face lit up. "Why don't we get Murphy to help? He was so great at guiding you two to Tawny in the first place. Maybe he can help sniff out Tawny's home!"

"That is such a great idea," said Kat. "Let's take Tawny back to my house. I'll ask my mom and we can call Aunt Jenn."

The girls hurried back to Kat's house with Tawny. Grace and Maya waited outside with Tawny while Kat went inside. In a moment, she was back. "Mom said she'll hold dinner until we're done, but said to be careful." Kat made a face. "Mom always says that. And Aunt Jenn says we can borrow Murphy! She's putting his leash on for us right now. She said she had a leash for Tawny, too. Let's go!"

The girls hurried to Tails Up. When they got there, Aunt Jenn was waiting outside with Murphy. As soon as the sheltie pup saw the girls and Tawny, he wagged his tail excitedly.

Tawny squirmed happily in Maya's arms. Maya put down the cocker spaniel so the dogs could greet each other.

"Here you go," Aunt Jenn said. She gave Murphy's leash to Kat. Then she handed her a pink leash. "For this little lost dog," she said, rubbing Tawny's head.

"Thanks, Aunt Jenn. You're the best!" Aunt Jenn was so kind, and she loved dogs so much. She always thought of everything. Kat wanted to be just like her when she grew up.

"I'll be here when you're done," Aunt Jenn said. "Good luck, girls. Good luck, Detective Murphy!"

"Thanks again, Aunt Jenn," Kat said. Then she turned to Maya and Grace, Tawny and Murphy. "Okay, let's hit the streets, gang. We're off to find Tawny's owner!"

CHAPTER EIGHT

The girls headed back up the street, into the park and across the field to the hill. Murphy tumbled along beside Kat, his head held high, his eyes sparkling. He seemed to sense they were on a mission. Although she did not have the same energy as the puppy, Tawny kept up well. *Maybe she knows she's going home,* thought Kat.

They circled the bottom of the hill until they

reached its far side. Now they were on the edge of their town. Several streets making up a small neighbourhood sprawled before them.

"Okay, when we stood up there, on top of the hill, and looked down, we saw Tawny's owner standing right here," said Kat. "When Tawny ran down the hill to her, they left together in that direction." Kat pointed down the street, to the east. "Right, Maya?"

"Right. So we'll begin by going that way," Maya said. "When we get close to her home, maybe Tawny will signal us in some way."

The girls walked on, watching to see if the cocker spaniel showed any interest in any of the houses they passed. But she didn't. Tawny looked here and there, but she was mainly interested in watching the puppy. And no wonder! Murphy snapped at the yellow head of a dandelion on a lawn. He grabbed a stick and marched along happily with it between his teeth. He stared as a flock of sparrows set flight from a tree branch.

At the end of the street, Tawny slowed in front of a two-storey brick home. There was a tricycle on the porch and a tire swing on the tree.

"Is this it, Tawny?" Maya asked, excitedly. "Is this your house?"

Tawny sat down on the edge of the lawn. Then she lay down.

As Kat stood examining the house, Murphy nudged the cocker spaniel curiously with his nose. When the older dog didn't move, the puppy flopped down beside her, snuggled up and closed his eyes.

The girls laughed.

"Maybe this isn't Tawny's house. Maybe both the dogs are just tired!" Kat said, giggling.

"Murphy's little puppy legs are probably exhausted," agreed Grace. "And Tawny has run around a lot today. She was in the park this afternoon, and then she walked halfway to Kat's house."

"Maybe, but I'll go and check anyway while the dogs rest up," said Maya. She strode toward the house.

Kat grinned admiringly. Maya was so confident!

Maya knocked on the door. A little girl opened it. They saw her look toward the cocker spaniel and the sheltie lying on her front lawn. Then she shook her head.

Maya came back. "Nope. Tawny's not their dog. The mom called out to me from the kitchen,

though. She said she's seen an older woman walking a cocker spaniel but she doesn't know exactly where she lives."

"So we're on the right track at least," said Kat. "And there are only two more streets."

Now both Tawny and Murphy jumped up. The little rest seemed to have given them new energy. Tawny swept her tail from side to side. Murphy pulled at the leash, ready for action.

"Okay, let's go, dogs," said Maya.

Off they went down the street. They walked around the corner and turned up the next street.

All of a sudden, Murphy began sniffing. He pulled them along toward a red picket fence that surrounded a small white house. His ears perked up. He began wagging his tail. Sniff, sniff, sniff!

"Murphy seems to recognize this smell," said Grace.

Murphy began pulling Kat along the fence

toward the front gate. It was standing open just enough to allow a small dog to push through.

"Look! The gate isn't closed properly. That's how Tawny got out!" said Maya.

"Her owner should make sure the gate is closed before she lets Tawny into the yard," said Grace firmly. "She isn't taking very good care of her dog."

"No, she isn't," said Maya, scowling.

The cocker spaniel was wagging her tail and pulling toward the house too. She seemed to know where she was.

Murphy sat by the gate, looking proud.

"Murphy, good pup! I think you've done it. I think you've found Tawny's home," said Kat. She bent down and smothered the sheltie in kisses. He wiggled happily.

"Well," said Maya, "I still don't know if we should take Tawny back. Not if her owner can't even keep her gate closed." She crossed her arms.

"Me, too," agreed Grace.

For a moment, Kat wished they'd never tried to find Tawny's home. She wished they'd thought about it longer, maybe overnight. Wouldn't it have been nice to fall asleep with the cocker spaniel curled up at the foot of her bed? Wouldn't it have been nice to wake up in the morning with Tawny there with her?

She looked down at the dog. The cocker spaniel continued to pull excitedly on the leash. Kat shook off the feeling of regret. Bringing Tawny home was obviously the right thing to do. She knew it.

"Tawny definitely wants to go home," Kat pointed out. "And besides, we don't know the whole story. We haven't even met Tawny's owner yet. Maybe . . . maybe there's something we can do to make things better for Tawny."

Maya and Grace considered Kat's words.

"Okay, that makes sense," Maya said. "Grace?"

Grace nodded. "Maybe you're right," she said.

The girls passed through the gate. Tawny was so excited she was almost pulling Grace down the path toward the house. Kat, last in line with Murphy, stopped to latch the gate behind them. But instead of walking on, Murphy whined and sat down.

"What's up, Murphy?" Kat asked. "What's wrong?"

Kat looked back. The gate had swung open.

Again Kat closed the gate and latched it. But now she realized that the latch was broken. It wouldn't hold for more than a second or so.

"You're so clever, Murphy," Kat said, reaching down to pat the puppy's head. "What a good boy!"

As Maya knocked on the front door, Kat told the girls about the latch.

"Well, why hasn't Tawny's owner taken the time to fix it?" Grace said, frustrated. "How much trouble could that be?"

"Exactly," agreed Maya.

The girls waited in silence for several minutes. Tawny whined expectantly. But there was no response.

"Maybe she's not home," said Grace.

Kat's heart began to thump. For a wonderful moment, she imagined taking Tawny back home for the night. Maybe they could even take her to the park with Murphy tomorrow after school!

Maya knocked again. Still, nothing.

"Guess we'll have to come back some other time," Grace said with a shrug.

"Well, good try, Murphy," Kat said to the puppy. "You led us right here, but there's no one home!"

The girls turned to go. But Grace said, "Oh, look. Tawny won't leave!" The cocker spaniel sat a few steps from the door, staring at it, refusing to budge as Grace gently pulled on the leash.

"We know this is your home," Grace said to her, "but your owner's not here. You have to come with us."

Now Tawny lay down. She put her head on her front paws and whined.

Kat felt terrible. Tawny was desperate to be back in her own home. Kat was sorry she'd ever hoped Tawny's owner wouldn't be here. What were they going to do?

Suddenly Murphy's ears swivelled toward the

front door. He gave a little bark and wagged his tail.

"No, Murphy. There's no one there," Kat told him.

But then she heard the faint sound of a woman's voice. "Yes? Yes, I'm coming!"

All of a sudden the front door opened.

CHAPTER NINE

A tall elderly woman was in the doorway. It was the same woman they had seen with Tawny that afternoon. Now she leaned on a cane. She peered this way and that.

"Tawny? Tawny, is that you?" the woman called.

Tawny danced about on the end of the leash, whining. Grace unclipped the leash, and the cocker spaniel lunged forward, pressing herself against the woman's legs.

"Oh, Tawny, it is you!" The woman bent down to pet her dog. "I'm so sorry. You've been out here a long time. Of course you want to come back in now." She paused. "But you didn't knock on the door, did you, Tawny. Of course not. I was certain I'd heard knocking . . ." She stood up holding Tawny.

Kat called out, "That was us knocking!"

She and Maya and Murphy headed back down the walkway toward the front door. They stopped beside Grace. "My name is Katherine, Kat for short," Kat explained. "These are my friends Maya and Grace. And this is Murphy.

He's a Shetland sheepdog puppy."

"Oh! I didn't see you girls there. Or your puppy. My eyes . . . well, they aren't what they used to be, that's for certain!" The woman smiled. "This is my cocker spaniel, Tawny." Tawny squirmed in her arms and barked. "Tawny, quiet! And I am Mrs. Borman, Ida Borman. How can I help you?"

"Well, we wanted to speak to you about Tawny," said Kat.

"Oh, my goodness." The woman's face fell. "What has my little rascal done now?"

"It's all right," said Kat quickly. "We like Tawny. She's a very sweet and friendly dog."

The woman smiled. "But how do you know her?" she asked. "Have we met before?"

"Um, yes and no," Kat said. She hesitated, unsure how to go on.

Maya stepped forward. "We were on the hill in the park this afternoon and we . . . well, Murphy really . . . found Tawny in the middle of the woods. She was lost. We brought Tawny out to the edge of the woods. Then we heard you calling, and Tawny ran to you. We saw you head off down the street with her, so we guessed that you must live in this neighbourhood."

"Oh my!" said Mrs. Borman. She clutched Tawny close to her.

"Then Tawny showed up near Kat's house about an hour ago, all by herself. It looked like she was lost again. So the three of us, and Murphy, brought her over here, hoping we could find your house. And, with Murphy's help, we did," Maya said.

"Murphy has been a hero, twice," said Grace softly. "Haven't you, Murphy?" She reached down and petted the puppy. He licked her hand.

"Well, good heavens!" Mrs. Borman shook her head again. "Thank you so much for bringing my Tawny back. I knew she ran away earlier, but I didn't know she was loose again just now.

And just the day before yesterday, a neighbour found her and brought her back. And once last week, as well."

Tears came to her eyes. "As you may realize," she said, "I don't see very well. My eyesight was never very good, but it has become worse in the last little while. I'm not completely blind, but my doctor told me I should consider getting a guide dog."

Suddenly Mrs. Borman chuckled. Brusquely, she wiped the tears away. "A guide dog! Can you imagine? How do you think my Tawny would like sharing me with another dog? She'd be jealous as all get-out!"

The girls laughed. Murphy wagged his tail.

"Well, I don't need a guide dog, but I must do something about Tawny. I want to keep her safe. If something ever happened to her, well . . ." Mrs. Borman shook her head. "But I don't know how she keeps getting out!"

Kat's heart melted. Mrs. Borman obviously loved her dog very much.

The girls exchanged a look. Kat could tell that Maya and Grace liked the woman, too.

"Mrs. Borman," said Maya carefully, "we think that Tawny's getting out through the front gate. When we got here, it wasn't latched."

"Not latched? Well, that can't be. I latch it every time I let Tawny out in the yard alone. I always close the gate!" Mrs. Borman said.

"The gate closes, but the latch is broken, so the gate swings open again," explained Kat.

A look of surprise crossed the woman's face. "Oh dear," she said. "Thank you so much for letting me know. I am very grateful. As soon as I go in, I'll arrange to have the latch fixed. And I certainly won't let Tawny out loose in the yard until it is!"

Grace smiled. "That's good," she said.

Mrs. Borman put her hand on her chest. "Thank you so much, girls," she said. Then her expression changed. "But it's not enough," she said. She looked thoughtful. She frowned. "It's not really enough."

The girls looked at each other in surprise. Not enough?

"I wonder," said Mrs. Borman. Now the woman was standing up straighter. She wasn't even leaning on her cane. "I think I know something else that would help. Would you girls be able to do one more thing for me?"

"Yes," said Kat quickly. "What is it?"

"Would you be able to help me out by walking Tawny once in a while?" Mrs. Borman suggested.

Kat let out a squeal of happiness. Maya's eyes opened wide. Grace bit her lip.

"*Could* we?" Kat breathed. "*Could* we walk Tawny?"

"I would appreciate it," Mrs. Borman said. "That is, if you have time. I know you already have a dog of your own . . ."

"Oh no, Murphy isn't ours. We're just looking after him." Kat explained that her aunt's grooming salon also boarded dogs. She told Mrs. Borman that she, Maya and Grace were helping out because they were crazy about dogs. "So we'd love to walk Tawny once in a while, too," said Kat. "Right, Maya? Grace?"

"Right," the two girls answered as one.

Mrs. Borman held Tawny close.

"Oh my, thank you again, girls," she said. "Thank you from the both of us. And if I can ever help any of you, please do let me know."

CHAPTER TEN

"How did it go?" asked Aunt Jenn.

"Murphy was amazing. He actually helped us to find Tawny's house!" said Kat. "Didn't you, puppy?" Kat scratched behind Murphy's ears and he wagged his tail happily.

"That's wonderful!" said Aunt Jenn. "Well, it's getting late. You girls should head home for dinner. I'll take Murphy inside. You'll come and walk him again tomorrow after school?"

"We sure will," agreed Kat. She, Maya and Grace said goodbye to Aunt Jenn. They headed up the street, chatting happily about their adventure.

When they got near the street that bordered the park, Grace suddenly stopped. "Well," she said uncertainly, gesturing toward the street. "My house is that way. I guess I'll see you tomorrow."

"Aren't you coming for dinner?" Kat asked. Then she remembered what had happened earlier. How Grace had overheard Maya talking about the Puppy Collection. Then Grace saying she had to go home for dinner.

"Listen, Grace," said Maya. "You should come. I'm sorry I've been rotten to you. It's just . . . hearing you talk about Bella, your dog . . . I was jealous. You've had a dog, and I'll probably never ever get one. Plus, I've never had to share my best friend before. It's not as easy as I thought. So I was mean to you." She bit her lip. Then she gave a half-smile. "Plus, if you don't come with us, I may be forced to listen to Kat-nip's jokes all by myself. No one should have to suffer through that alone."

Kat pretended to be offended. Then she turned and winked at Grace. Grace grinned.

"So, do you forgive me, Grace? You should. First, because I'm irresistible. And second, because if you do, you'll get to help us with our Puppy Collection, right, Kat?" Maya said.

Kat's eyes widened. Quickly, she nodded. "Yes! That's right!" she agreed.

"So, come on. What do you say?" Maya said, taking Grace's arm.

Grace blushed. "Well, okay," she agreed. "But, what exactly is the Puppy Collection?"

Kat and Maya explained it to Grace as they walked to Kat's house. And then, right after dinner, they hurried up to Kat's room to show Grace the scrapbook.

"This is Bailey," said Kat. She pointed to a photo of a chocolate brown Labrador retriever pup. "Look at his beautiful green eyes. He was the first puppy we looked after for Aunt Jenn. He was adorable."

"In our Puppy Collection, we put in a few photos or drawings of the puppy," explained Maya. "And a description, too."

She read out Bailey's note: *"Bailey is a Labrador retriever. He is eight weeks old. He is being house-trained, and he is doing well! Bailey likes to chase toys and shake them. He is very gentle. He likes to give us kisses."*

"And here's Riley. You remember her from the park last week, right?" said Kat.

"Oh, what a great photo of her. She was so sweet!" said Grace.

"And this is a picture that Kat drew of her," said Maya.

Kat didn't like showing people her drawings. She didn't think she was a good artist and she worried others would laugh. But Grace didn't.

"She has dark brown eyes just like that," said Grace admiringly.

Maya read out the description of Riley: *"Riley is a three-month-old golden retriever. She likes to bark at ants! She is learning to sit, lie down and come. She has a beautiful puppy smell."*

"Hey, I know you both have to go home soon," said Kat. "But let's make some notes about Murphy."

"Great idea!" agreed Maya. "And I'll bring my camera tomorrow and take a photo of him."

"And maybe you can do a drawing of him, Kat," Grace suggested.

Kat grinned. "Sure," she said.

"But first, there is something much, much more important that needs to be done," Maya announced dramatically.

The two girls looked at her blankly.

"Kat, comedienne extraordinaire? You must tell us a joke," said Maya. "How can we go on without a Kat-nip joke?"

Grace clapped. "Of course! Yes, Kat, a joke! We need a joke!"

Kat stuck out her tongue at her friends. "If you insist." She thought for a moment, then she said, "What do dogs have that no other animals have?"

Maya and Grace looked at each other. They shook their heads. "Don't know," Maya said. "What?"

"Are you ready for this?" Kat asked. "Hold your sides. Okay, what do dogs have that no other animals have? Puppies!"

It was hard to tell who groaned louder, Grace or Maya.

"You asked for it!" Kat told them, shaking her finger at them.

"We sure did," Maya agreed, throwing herself on Kat's bed and pretending to roll around in pain. "But we never imagined it could be as bad as that, did we Grace?"

"Never," said Grace, trying to hide her giggles. "Never!"

Kat sat and smiled, watching her two friends. It was a perfect ending to the day. Just perfect.

Bijou Needs a Home

*For lovely, lively Leah Witten and her
rambunctious poodle Santo*

CHAPTER ONE

Kat giggles. There are puppies everywhere! Some are tumbling in the grass. Some are chasing butterflies. Some are playing in the flower beds.

Some puppies are white, some are brown, some are red with spots. There are dachshunds and Afghans. There are Boston terriers and cocker spaniels.

There are too many puppies to count!

"Hey, Kat!" a voice said. "It's for you."

"Hey, Kat!" her brother Aidan says. "They're for you, Sis. Any puppy you want. Mom and Dad have finally agreed." He punches her gently on the shoulder.

Kat grins. She can't believe it! It's a dream come true.

But which one should she pick? The sweet black and white border collie with the sparkling eyes? The Bernese mountain dog pup wagging its roly-poly body? The cute Labrador retriever with the white star on its black tummy?

"Hey, Kat!" It was her brother's voice again. "Sis!"

Kat was sitting at the computer in the living room. It was Saturday. Kat had been looking at photos of different breeds of puppies on the computer until she began daydreaming.

"Earth to Kat," her brother said, handing the phone to her. "It's for you. It's Aunt Jenn."

Kat's favourite daydream in the world ended.

In real life she wasn't allowed to get a puppy. Her parents said they didn't have enough time to look after puppies.

But she was happy her aunt was phoning her. Aunt Jenn was the best. She loved dogs as much as Kat did. She had opened up a dog-grooming salon in town. Her business was called Tails Up! Grooming and Boarding and it was doing really well — better than she had thought it would. In fact, Aunt Jenn had just hired someone to help answer the phone and make appointments. But even with her new office helper, Aunt Jenn was still busy, busy, busy. So she often asked Kat to give her a hand. Most times Kat got her best friend, Maya, and her new friend, Grace, to come along. They usually helped Aunt Jenn with puppies that were boarding at Tails Up.

Kat grabbed the phone from Aidan. "Hi, Aunt Jenn!" she said.

"Hi, Kitty-Kat," said Aunt Jenn, using her

special name for Kat. "Listen, I wonder if you can help me out. Things are usually busy here on Saturdays. But this morning, there is an extra challenge."

"Sure," said Kat. "What is it? Has someone left a puppy to board with you? Does he need a walk or a play in the yard?"

"Well, something like that — times three!" Aunt Jenn laughed. "This morning I came downstairs to the salon early to prepare for another day of business. I opened the main door to pick up the newspaper, and what did I find? A big cardboard box — with three little white bichon frise puppies in it!" Aunt Jenn said. Now her voice sounded a bit upset.

Kat gasped. "Three abandoned puppies?"

"Yes," Aunt Jenn said. She sighed. "I think they are about eight weeks old. I put them in a kennel in the doggy-daycare room, and I gave them food and water. They need more attention, but I'm so busy today. It's almost noon, and this is the first chance I've even had to call you. You don't mind helping out this afternoon?"

"Of course not!" Kat said quickly. "Is it okay if

Maya and Grace come? We all love helping out at Tails Up. You know how dog crazy we are!"

"That would be wonderful," Aunt Jenn said. "That way there would be three of them and three of you!"

"I'll check with Mom and Dad," said Kat. "Then I'll call Maya and Grace."

"Oh, and Kitty-Kat, can you bring along poster-making supplies? It would be great if you could make posters advertising that the three pups need homes," suggested Aunt Jenn.

"Sure thing," said Kat. "See you in a flash. Or sooner!"

CHAPTER TWO

Fifteen minutes later, Maya and her mom pulled up in front of Kat's house. Maya leaned out the passenger window.

"Hi, Kat-nip," she called.

Kat made a face. Maya had called her "Kat-nip" for as long as she could remember. "You love dogs, but your name is Kat? How goofy!" she'd say. Maya often teased her, and Kat teased her back. But it was all in good fun.

They had been best friends forever.

Maya waved Kat over. "I told my mom that your aunt needs us yesterday," Maya said, grinning, "so she's going to give us a lift to Tails Up."

Kat jumped into the back seat. "Thanks, Mrs. Berg."

"You're welcome, Katherine," Maya's mother answered.

"What about Grace? Is she meeting us there?" Maya asked as Kat did up her seatbelt.

"Yup. In a while," Kat explained, "after a doctor's appointment. Oh, and she's going to bring along some art supplies for the posters."

Five minutes later, Maya's mother dropped off the girls in front of Tails Up. The grooming salon was on the main street of Orchard Valley, just a few blocks from Kat's house.

The girls hurried inside. A young man sitting behind the front desk waved. "Hello, girls," he said. "You're Kat? And you're Maya? I'm Tony, the new receptionist," he explained, standing up.

"Hi, Tony," said Maya.

"Nice to meet you," said Kat.

"And this is Marmalade. She's fifteen. She won't go anywhere without me." Tony grinned.

A big, elderly tabby cat was sitting on the countertop.

"Hi, Marmalade," Kat said.

"Can we pet her?" Maya asked.

"Go ahead," Tony said. "But don't think for a moment that she'll enjoy it. She'll allow it but only as a favour to you!" He winked at them.

Kat and Maya stroked the elderly cat, and sure enough, she didn't look at them. But she purred loudly.

The phone rang. "Your aunt should be out in a minute," Tony said, before answering the phone with a cheerful "Tails Up! How can I help you?"

Kat looked around the waiting room. As always, it was packed. It had a small couch and three chairs. Today almost every seat was taken. A bald man sat with a stocky bull terrier lying at his feet. A teenage girl with a shaved head, five earrings in one ear and one in her bottom lip held her Great Dane on a short leash. It had black studs on its collar. It wagged its tail happily at Kat and Maya.

A young woman sat sprawled on a chair. She wore a trim jacket and skirt, and black boots.

She had long, black hair in tight curls that cascaded down her back.

Maya nudged Kat and tilted her head toward the young woman.

Kat studied her. What breed of dog would she have? This was one of Kat and Maya's favourite games.

"Puli," Kat whispered to Maya, after a moment.

"Puli?" Maya frowned. "Okay, Einstein. What's a puli?"

"It's a really rare dog breed," Kat began to explain. "Pulis look really unusual, like moving mops! They have—"

Just then, Aunt Jenn came bounding out of the grooming studio. As usual, her brown hair was pulled back into a ponytail. She wore a light blue jacket sprinkled with black, brown, tan and red dog hairs. Beside her bounced a black dog with long cords of tightly curled hair that touched the ground. When he moved, the cords swung back and forth.

"Cocoa!" The young woman bent down to greet her dog. "You good boy!" Her own curls bounced up and down.

"Cocoa's a puli!" Kat said, grinning.

Maya gasped in surprise. "And his owner has a matching hairdo! Nice one, Kat."

Aunt Jenn turned to the waiting clients. "I just need a minute to speak with my niece and her friend. I'll be right back," she said firmly.

"Hello, wonderful girls," she said to Kat and Maya. "Thank you so much for coming!" She waved them to follow her into the doggy-daycare room.

It had a large fenced-in area, like a playpen. There was a stairway that led to a big room for puppy training and Aunt Jenn's apartment. There was a window looking onto a big fenced-in yard. There were also four large dog kennels along one wall. In the closest one were three little white puppies. When they saw the girls, two of the puppies jumped up and began wagging their tails.

"Here they are," said Aunt Jenn. "The bichon frise pups!"

Kat and Maya squealed with delight and hurried over. They dropped to their knees beside the kennel.

"They are so sweet!" cooed Kat.

"They are so tiny!" exclaimed Maya.

"Two females and one male," Aunt Jenn said, pointing out which was which.

"It's hard to tell them apart," said Maya. "All three are white and so cute!"

"The male looks a little smaller than the females," Kat said thoughtfully. "And he seems a little quieter." The male puppy sat in the corner and watched his sisters play together.

"Likely they are siblings from one litter," said Aunt Jenn. "There may have been others in the litter. Perhaps the owner found homes for the others, but not for these three puppies, and so he or she left them here."

"But why?" Kat said angrily. She stood up. "Why would anyone just abandon a box of puppies outside a grooming salon?"

"And what if you hadn't found them right away?" Maya added, her eyes flashing. "What if the pups had climbed out of the box and run onto the street?"

"These are good questions," said Aunt Jenn. "We'll never know who put the puppies outside Tails Up or why. But the good news is that these three little ones are safe and sound!"

"True," Maya said.

Kat nodded. Aunt Jenn was right.

"So your job this afternoon is to play with them while I work." Aunt Jenn stuck her finger in the air. "And also to come up with an action plan. We need to find each one a home — and quickly! These pups are about eight weeks old. They will begin to bond with the people around them. So they need to be with their forever family as soon as possible. We don't want them to bond with us! It would be too difficult for them to separate from us."

Kat swallowed hard. She stared at the puppies. What if they couldn't find homes for all three puppies? What if one pup was left behind and never found his or her forever family?

She forced herself to put the feeling aside. They would just have to do their best to see that didn't happen.

CHAPTER THREE

"You're okay with these three pups? You don't need any reminders on how to lift them out of the kennel or place them back in?" Aunt Jenn asked.

"No, we're fine," said Kat with a smile.

"Good," Aunt Jenn said. She turned to go, but then turned back. "Almost forgot. Names!" she said. "We need to be able to tell the puppies apart when we're talking about them. Can you take care of naming them all?"

Kat paused. "But won't that make them bond with us too much, Aunt Jenn?"

Aunt Jenn shook her head. "Don't think so. Many breeders name their puppies and then the new owners rename them. Puppies learn their new names quickly. I have several books about dogs in my waiting room, including ones filled with names. Help yourself." With one more grin at the girls, she was gone.

Kat's head was swimming. She looked at Maya. "What do we do first?"

Maya slapped her hand to her chest. "Oh, woe is us," she said dramatically. "Decisions, decisions, decisions . . ."

Kat giggled. Her best friend would make a great actress!

"But seriously, Maya, what do we do first?" Kat said. She knelt beside the kennel. Two of the puppies tumbled over to her excitedly. Kat longed to play with them all.

"Well, how about we talk about the posters first," said Maya.

Kat turned back to the puppies. "We're going to make posters to tell people about you three," she told them. The two puppies wagged their tails excitedly. The third pup stayed in the corner, just watching.

"We'll put up posters around town, and we can put them up at school on Monday, as well," said Maya.

"Okay," said Kat. "We'll write on the posters that these puppies will only go to responsible people. People who will take good care of them and love them forever."

"Sounds good," Maya agreed. "Now, while we wait for Grace to come with the poster supplies, why don't we play with the pups?"

"Great idea!" said Kat.

Maya hurried over to join Kat by the crate.

"The male is a little smaller, but the two

females are exactly the same size," Maya said, looking at the puppies. "Spunky and lively. White with black noses and black button eyes. It's hard to tell them apart."

Kat looked back and forth, back and forth at the females. "You're right," she agreed. "Identical."

"You know what?" Maya said, looking at them closely. "I think there is one difference, after all. Neither of them actually has black eyes. *She* has eyes that are almost black." She pointed to the pup on the left. "But *her* eyes are dark brown!"

Kat peered at the puppies, then smiled. "You're right, Maya!"

Kat opened the kennel and reached in. The two females came right over. They looked up at Kat and licked her fingers happily.

"Okay, you first, little one," Kat said. Gently she lifted up the puppy with the almost black eyes. She hugged the squirming puffball against her chest.

"You are adorable," Kat said, softly. "Just adorable."

She stroked the puppy's soft coat. She liked how her tail curled up over her back, just like the top of a question mark.

Maya lifted out the other female puppy.

"Oh, she is so tiny!" Maya said. "I don't think I've ever held such a little puppy!"

"It's almost like holding a stuffed toy dog, isn't it?" Kat exclaimed. "Except these puppies are real!"

Kat cuddled the puppy for a few more minutes. Then she set her down. "Time to play!" At once the curious female began to explore the room. She sniffed the three other kennels, which were empty. She found a basket of dog toys. She pulled out a plush squirrel. She held it between her teeth and shook her head from side to side.

Kat laughed. "The squirrel is almost as big as the puppy!"

Maya set the other puppy down. She ran

to join her sister. The two bichon frise pups began to play a happy game of tug-of-war.

Kat looked at the male puppy. He still sat in the corner of the kennel. He was watching his sisters closely. He didn't look nervous or scared, just cautious.

"Your turn to come out," Kat told him. She put her hand in the kennel. The puppy approached it slowly. He sniffed Kat's hand. Then, quick as a wink, out came his pink tongue to give her hand a gentle lick.

"Thank you," said Kat, feeling especially pleased. "Nice to meet you, too. Now here we go," she said and picked him up. He was so soft. Kat held the puppy close against her chest. She could feel his heart thumping. He was even tinier than his sisters.

Suddenly Kat was worried. The puppies were very sweet, but it might be difficult to find owners for all three. Especially in only a few days. Especially if one puppy acted a little shy. What would happen if they couldn't find someone who would love each puppy forever? What would happen to this little fellow if they couldn't find someone who wanted to take him home?

CHAPTER FOUR

The door opened and Grace peeked her head in.

"Kat? Maya?" she called.

"Hi, Grace," replied Kat. "Come in quickly and close the door behind you. The puppies are loose!"

Grace quickly slipped into the room. "Hi, guys! Sorry I'm late," she said. Grace caught sight of the three puppies. "Oh my goodness!" she cooed. She whipped off her backpack and dropped the art supplies by the door.

"Look at you cute little things!"

Kat remembered the first time she saw Grace. It was just a short time ago. Grace had just moved to Orchard Valley. She was put in Kat's grade four/five class. She stood at the front of the room with their teacher, Ms. Mitchell. She didn't smile. Her arms were straight down at her sides. Her face was stony.

At first Kat thought Grace was just . . . mean. That's what all the other kids in the class thought, too. But Kat had been helping Aunt Jenn look after a puppy called Riley. And Riley had taught her that Grace was just missing her own dog and her own home. Grace looked mean when she was scared or embarrassed.

Now Grace squatted on the floor. The two female pups were chasing a ball across the floor. But when they saw the girl crouching there, they hurried over to her, their legs flying. They jumped up at her like jack-in-the-boxes.

"Bichons are really great at doing tricks. In the past they performed in circuses," said Kat, grinning.

Kat read about dogs on the Internet. She read every dog book she could get her hands on. Her favourite book was *Dog Breeds of the World.* She must have read it more than twenty times. She wanted to learn everything she could about dogs.

Grace clapped her hands together. "I can believe it! Just look at these two prance and pirouette!" She patted one puppy with each hand. "Hello, my friends!" Then she looked at the male puppy. "And what about this little one?" He was happily chewing on a squeaky toy. "Come on over and see me," Grace coaxed. "Come on." She stretched out a hand to the puppy. He wagged his tail, but he stayed where he was. His sisters jumped at Grace's hand, wanting the attention back on them.

"So, first things first," said take-charge Maya. "Grace, we have to find names for these three. I'll get the books Aunt Jenn mentioned."

Maya hurried out to the waiting room and returned with the books. She passed them out. Then she pulled out some paper and a pen from the bag of art supplies.

"I'll be the recorder," Maya said. "Okay, anytime you find a good name, call it out, and I'll write it down."

The girls settled into the brainstorming session. Kat sat on the floor near the male puppy. She found a section in her book on names for male dogs. As she looked through the names, she tugged on the squeaky toy. The puppy pulled back on the toy, his head down and his rear end up in the air. She liked his fierce little growling sounds.

"How about Snowball?" suggested Grace. She flicked the end of one of her long red braids. "Or Snowflake?"

"Good. I'll write those down," said Maya.

"Puff?" Grace added.

"You know," said Kat thoughtfully, "the name bichon frise is French, and it actually means *curly lap dog.*"

"Perfect!" Grace laughed. "I bet I could fit both these pups in my lap at once!"

"So, maybe it would be a good idea to give these puppies French names," suggested Kat.

"Mais oui!" cried Maya. "That's a great idea!"

Grace smiled, but it was difficult for Kat to tell if she agreed or not. She didn't often tell the girls what she was thinking. *Grace is a little like the third bichon frise puppy,* Kat thought with a grin. *A bit quiet. A bit cautious.*

Kat wondered if Grace was like that with everyone. Or was it just with her and Maya? Kat had become friends with Grace first. Then she had introduced her to Maya. The two of them were getting along all right now, but the other kids at school still didn't seem to know what to make of Grace. Kat hoped Grace would make more new friends soon.

She sighed. For some reason, friendship was definitely not easy. And sometimes kids at school seemed to make things even harder. *Dogs seem to make friends a lot easier than people do,* Kat thought.

Just then, the male puppy picked up the squeaky toy and trotted to the other side of the room. He flopped down and curled up with the toy, all alone.

Except for this guy, that is, Kat thought. *He doesn't seem to want to make friends with us!*

"So come on, girls," Maya said impatiently. "Names! We need names! And in French, *si'l vous plaît!*" Maya made googly eyes. "That means *please*, for those who don't understand French as well as *moi*!"

Kat and Grace giggled. Soon the names were

flying. Maya listed them all.

While the girls worked, the two female puppies fell asleep near the basket of toys — one on top of the other, exhausted from their exploring, running and tugging. The male puppy snoozed, tucked up against his squeaky toy.

"Okay," announced Maya after a while. "I think we have a long enough list."

Maya read out the names one by one, and the girls voted for the names they liked best. Grace jotted down the scores.

"Now for the results," said Maya after doing a tally. "First, the female with the deep, dark eyes. She will be Aimée, which means *loved*. The female with the chocolate brown eyes is Chantal. I don't know what it means, but it sounds so pretty. *Chantal, Chantal!*" repeated Maya, grinning. "And the male? Say *bonjour* to Bijou, which means *jewel*."

"Perfect," said Grace. "I love these names."

"Me, too." Kat smiled, delighted.

CHAPTER FIVE

Grace pulled out the markers, pens, paper and bristol boards. The girls talked about what to write on the posters so they could find good homes for the puppies.

"Must be kind and loving," suggested Maya.

"Must be willing to go on walks — rain or snow," said Grace.

"Must need a very special friend," added Kat, looking at Bijou.

Then, all at once the puppies woke up. Right away, they were on the go! Chantal scooted to the corner of the room and peed. With a happy yip, Aimée pounced on a marker that had fallen to the floor. And Bijou decided to try to chew open a bag of dog biscuits that Aunt Jenn had set by the back door.

The girls decided to take turns playing with the puppies and making the posters. As they worked, Aunt Jenn came into the doggy-daycare room.

"How's it going in here?" Aunt Jenn asked. She popped a piece of gum in her mouth. "How are the little ones?"

"We've named the puppies Aimée, Chantal and Bijou," explained Kat. "We're making posters and we're going to post them up and down the main street and at school!"

"Wonderful!" exclaimed Aunt Jenn. "Please put the Tails Up telephone number on the posters. Tony can arrange for us to meet with any interested callers."

She grinned as Aimée and Chantal came tumbling toward her. "I hope there are three families out there who want new puppies — and soon! These scallywags really need to be with their own people soon."

Aunt Jenn squatted down. The two fluffy white puppies covered her hand in kisses. "But I'm sure we won't have any trouble once they meet them. These two certainly are hard to resist!" she laughed.

Kat looked at Bijou, who was sitting watching his sisters. He had his head cocked to one side. *What about him?* Kat wondered. *Will Bijou be friendly enough to get a family of his own?*

It gave her a funny feeling. Part of her wanted the puppy to be left behind. Maybe she could convince her parents to let her bring him home! But another part of her knew that wasn't possible. And if no one wanted him, what would happen to the sweet little guy?

Kat shuddered and put the thought out of her head.

"I must get back to my clients," said Aunt Jenn, standing up again. "Now, girls, when you leave, please make sure the puppies are safely back in their kennel." Aunt Jenn blew a pink bubble with her gum. "Also, Kitty-Kat, could you, Maya and Grace come after school on Monday and help out with these three again? That is, if they're all still here."

"Sure," said Kat. She looked at Maya and Grace, who both nodded enthusiastically.

"Lovely. Well then, ta-ta!" Aunt Jenn said cheerily. And off she went.

CHAPTER SIX

All morning and all afternoon, Kat couldn't stop thinking about Bijou. She sat in class at her desk with her math questions in front of her. But she didn't see numbers. Instead she saw a cute little white bichon frise chewing on a squeaky toy. She saw him cuddled up across the room, sleeping. She saw him looking at her, his head cocked to one side, cautious.

Kat looked at the clock. She sighed. The hands

did not seem to be moving very quickly today.

Come on, she told herself. *Just focus. Do your assignment. It might make the time go by faster.*

She bent over her math questions and began to work.

When she looked up again, the hands on the clock had moved. Finally.

Kat grinned and looked at Grace, who sat at the desk beside her. Grace was pulling at one of her braids and staring into space. Her paper was blank.

"Hey," Kat whispered. "I know what you're thinking about."

Grace smiled back at her.

"Bichon frise puppies? And the interviews?

Grace nodded.

"All right, class," said Ms. Mitchell. She stood at the front of the room. Behind her, on the blackboard, she had written the same math questions that were on their papers. "Now, I need some brave souls to come up and show us their work. But I'm not going to ask for volunteers this time." She looked around. "Owen, Cara, Lindsay, Grace. Come up, please."

Grace shot Kat a panicked look. She didn't move from her seat while the other children got up and went to the board.

"Grace, you have to go," Kat told her. She gave her shoulder a gentle push.

"I can't do it," Grace said. She flushed.

"That's okay. Just go and try," Kat suggested.

"I'll get them all wrong," Grace said.

"Ms. Mitchell will help you," Kat told her.

Someone snickered from behind. It was Megan. She sat behind Grace.

Kat turned around and glared at Megan. Megan rolled her eyes, like she thought Grace was stupid. It wasn't the first time. Megan had been mean to Grace from the start.

Kat decided not to say anything. It might just

encourage Megan. That's what Kat's mom said sometimes when she was arguing with Aidan. Megan snickered again, and Grace must have heard her. Grace had that mean look on her face. Her face looked like stone. Kat knew it meant Grace was embarrassed or uncomfortable. It didn't mean she was going to do something nasty. It didn't even mean she was thinking unpleasant thoughts. That was the thing you had to know about Grace. How she looked didn't

often equal how she felt. It wasn't like a math question.

Grace got up and began walking to the board.

"The new girl. What's her name again?" Megan said, pretending she'd forgotten. She spoke just loud enough so Kat and Grace could hear.

Grace kept walking. Her arms were straight down at her sides.

She picked up the chalk and she looked at the math questions, but she didn't write anything.

Just at Kat had predicted, Ms. Mitchell came and stood beside her. She talked to Grace in a soft voice, pointing at the numbers, explaining what to do. In only a few minutes, Grace was filling in all the answers, and they were correct.

When the end-of-day bell rang, Kat and Grace hurried out to meet Maya.

"That Megan is so mean," Kat said to Grace.

Grace didn't reply.

"I should say something to her. Defend you,"

suggested Kat. "Tell Ms. Mitchell she's bothering you. Or . . . do something mean to her. Take revenge. That's what Maya always says, and maybe she's right . . ." Kat didn't like the idea but maybe it would work.

"No!" Grace said. She turned to Kat and put her hand on her arm, stopping her. "No. Don't."

"But . . ." Kat stopped. She could see tears in Grace's eyes.

"Don't. Please," Grace insisted.

"Okay," agreed Kat. "I won't."

Maya was waiting at the usual spot.

"So?" she asked, as they headed down the street toward the grooming salon. "Let's have it. Joke of the day. You forgot to tell us one this morning before school."

Grace slapped her forehead and tried not to grin. "And I thought I'd escaped."

"No, it is a tradition that we must endure," said

Maya. "Come on now, Kat-nip. Hit us with one."

Kat thought for a moment. "What do you get if you cross a sheepdog with a rose?" she asked.

"I don't know," said Maya.

"Me neither," said Grace.

"A cauliflower!" cried Kat. "Get it? A collie-flower?"

"Oh! So bad," moaned Maya.

"So, so bad," echoed Grace. "Worst ever."

Kat started to laugh. But just then Megan and Cora rode by on their bikes.

"Kat and Owen sitting in a tree," they chanted. "K-I-S-S-I-N-G."

The two girls didn't even look at Kat. But Kat knew they meant her to hear them. That Megan. Take the *g* out of her name and it spelled *mean*.

Maya frowned. "I thought they stopped teasing you after you stood up to them," she said to Kat.

"Yeah, well, they started again," Kat said. She shrugged. She tried to pretend it didn't bother

her. She hoped they weren't teasing Owen, too. He wasn't her boyfriend, but he was nice.

Soon the girls reached Aunt Jenn's salon. Inside it was as crowded as usual. Tony looked up, gave a friendly wave, and then went back to typing on the computer. Marmalade stuck her tail up in the air and pretended the girls weren't there.

Kat stroked Marmalade's back anyway. "You can't fool me," she whispered into the tabby cat's ear.

Then Kat led Maya and Grace past the five clients: a border collie, two Pomeranians, a West Highland terrier and a Doberman.

Kat paused with her hand on the door to the doggy-daycare room. What if one or two of the puppies were gone? What if Bijou wasn't there?

CHAPTER SEVEN

Kat breathed a sigh of relief. All three of the puppies were still there. Kat wanted the puppies to find homes, but she didn't want them to leave without saying goodbye! And of course Aunt Jenn wouldn't let that happen. Not even if the puppies did find homes.

The girls put down their backpacks and hurried over to the kennel.

"Hello, Chantal. *Bonjour!*" said Maya, lifting

out the brown-eyed puppy. Chantal licked Maya's cheeks and wiggled with excitement.

"Now you, Aimée. Out you come," said Grace. She gave the snow-white puppy a quick kiss on her tiny head.

"And you too, Bijou," murmured Kat. The puppy wagged his curled-up tail while she held him close. He was being so friendly. Maybe he remembered her! Kat smelled his lovely puppy smell. She stroked his soft coat.

"Play time!" announced Kat. When the girls set down the puppies, Chantal and Aimée scampered toward each other and began to wrestle. Bijou, however, had other things on his mind. He headed over to the toy basket and found a small plastic ball. He tried to bite it, but it was much too large for him to get a grip. It rolled away, and he chased it and tried again.

"Those sisters are going to miss each other," said Maya, watching them tussle. "But this one?"

Maya added, pointing to Bijou. "Not so much. He's a bit of a loner, isn't he?"

The time went quickly. The girls knew they had to make the most of it. Perhaps all the puppies would have new homes by tomorrow!

Maya and Grace played with Aimée and Chantal. They sat on the floor across from each other with the puppies in between them. They rolled a soccer ball back and forth to each other. The puppies ran back and forth too, chasing the ball. A few times, Chantal was so excited she almost did a somersault. Aimée kept skidding into the girls' legs, unable to stop in time.

Bijou seemed happy playing alone, but Kat was worried. "You need to be able to socialize," she whispered to him. "It's important. Most people get dogs because they want to play with them. You won't get chosen if you don't seem very friendly."

Kat took Bijou's ball and threw it for him, but he wouldn't chase it.

He headed back to the toy basket and picked out a toy bone. He growled and shook it in his mouth.

Kat laughed. "Here, bring it here!" she said, crouching down and patting the floor. "Bring it to me!" But Bijou didn't come. He didn't even look at her.

Kat got a real dog biscuit from the bag that was now up on the shelf. She sat down across from Bijou.

"Look, Bijou! A biscuit for you!" she said,

trying to tempt him. "Come here. Come here
and you can have it."

Bijou dropped the toy bone.

"Here you go. Good puppy!" Kat said
encouragingly.

Bijou turned and went back to the toy basket
to look for another toy.

Kat looked at Maya and Grace. They were
both lying on their backs giggling, and Chantal
and Aimée were climbing up and over them.

"Your little paws are as light as feathers,
Chantal!" giggled Maya.

"Oh, that tickles!" squealed Grace, as Aimée
scampered across her tummy.

Kat sighed. Bijou had found a new toy and
was happily chewing at it, all by himself.

Suddenly Maya cried out, "Oh! I almost forgot!" She gently pushed Chantal off her stomach and got up. "I brought my camera!" She went to her backpack and took it out.

"Good!" said Kat, jumping up as well. "We can add Chantal, Aimée and Bijou to our Puppy Collection!"

Maya began snapping photos of Chantal, who was trying to spring up onto Grace's belly. Then Grace sat up and set Aimée on the floor. Maya took photos of the puppy as she yipped and chased her sister, Chantal, across the room.

"These photos will be perfect for the Puppy Collection," Grace said.

Maya and Kat had started the Puppy Collection together just a short time ago. Neither girl was allowed to have a dog, so they did the next best thing. They drew pictures of their favourite puppies or they took photos of them. They gave each puppy a name and wrote a description of it. They also added puppies they met, such as the ones they helped to look after at Tails Up. Now that Grace was their friend, she helped with the Puppy Collection, too.

"Don't forget to take some photos of Bijou," Kat reminded Maya.

"Why don't you pick him up?" suggested Maya. "I'll take one of both of you."

Kat was happy to scoop up the puppy. But when she tried to get him to look at the camera, he only wanted to gaze at her quietly with his dark brown button eyes. She looked back at him, her heart melting.

A while later, it was time to go. The girls put the puppies back in the kennel and said good night to them. They grabbed their backpacks and closed the door to the doggy daycare behind them.

Just then Aunt Jenn came hurrying down the hall.

"Ah, good. You're still here! Can't chat long. I still have two more dogs to groom." She pulled out her ponytail and made a new one. "But I wanted to tell you that I've set up an interview with someone keen to adopt one of our puppies. Would you girls be able to come and sit in on it? It's tomorrow after school."

Kat's heart sank, but she knew it was a good thing. The puppies needed their own homes as soon as possible.

"Sure thing," said Kat firmly. "I can come."

"Not me," Maya said. She made a face. "I have my piano lesson tomorrow."

"I'll be here." Grace nodded enthusiastically. I can help."

"Thank you," said Aunt Jenn. She flashed them a smile. "See you tomorrow, then. And now, I'm off!"

CHAPTER EIGHT

School was over for the day. Kat stood in the school entranceway waiting for Grace. Kat was looking at one of the posters they had put up the previous morning. *What's going to happen after school today?* Kat wondered. Three puppies but only one interview.

"Tails Up. Um . . . isn't that your aunt's grooming and boarding place?"

Kat jumped. She hadn't noticed that Owen

was standing beside her reading the poster. She had been daydreaming again.

"Yes," she said.

He blushed. She didn't know why.

"Does she let me . . . you, I mean . . ." He frowned. He took a breath. "Does she let you come and pay . . . I mean, play with the dogs sometimes?" he asked.

Kat tried not to smile. "Yes, she does," she told him.

Maya was certain Owen got tongue-tied around Kat because he liked her. Megan and Cora thought so, too. A short time ago, they had teased Kat about it and even written her a note with hearts on it. *Dreaming about Owen?* Of course Kat had been daydreaming about puppies, not Owen. Owen was her friend, not her boyfriend. Kat didn't mind Maya teasing her, but it wasn't okay for Megan and Cora to do it. They were trying to annoy her. They only stopped when they thought she was going to show their note to Ms. Mitchell. They didn't want to get in trouble with their teacher.

They aren't picking on me as much as they used to. But Megan seems to be teasing Grace more than ever, Kat thought, remembering how Megan had acted yesterday. *And today she pretended to forget Grace's name again. Which is just plain mean.*

"That must be fun," said Owen.

Kat looked at him blankly. Megan, being teased . . .

"Playing with the dogs. At Tails Up," Owen added.

"Oh, yes. Yes, it is!" Kat said, hastily. "In fact, I'm waiting for Grace and then we're going there. To Tails Up. Ms. Mitchell wanted to speak to her first."

Owen nodded. He wasn't looking at Kat anymore. He was looking at the poster. He didn't speak for a moment. Had he run out of things to say? Kat wondered.

"You seem to love dogs so much," Owen said. When he said the word *love*, he blushed again.

Kat didn't know why, but she blushed, too. "I do," Kat agreed. "Love dogs, I mean." She felt stupid for blushing. What was wrong with her?

Then Sunjit called out from down the hall, "O-wen. Come on, O. We're heading out." He was bouncing a basketball.

Thank goodness. Kat had never felt so awkward. Especially with a friend.

"Well, bye," said Owen. He put on his hat with the earflaps. He wore it all the time.

Kat grinned. She and Maya thought it made Owen look like a basset hound!

"See you," said Kat.

Owen stood for a moment without moving.

"O-wen. Come on!" yelled Sunjit.

"Bye," said Owen again. He headed down

the hall toward his friend.

Just then Grace appeared.

"Sorry about that!" she said breathlessly. "Ms. Mitchell made some math sheets for me. She wanted to go over a few problems with me, too." Grace put on her backpack.

"Did you tell Ms. Mitchell about Megan? That she's been mean to you?" asked Kat, as they headed outside.

"No." Grace shook her head. "But I think she noticed yesterday, when I went up to the board to do the math problems. She asked me if I wanted her to talk to Megan."

"Oh, that's great," said Kat with relief. "That'll show Megan that she can't treat you that way."

Grace shrugged. "Well, not really."

"What do you mean?" Kat asked.

"I said no. I said I would work it out myself," Grace said.

Kat stared at her. "You're kidding," she said.

"No," Grace said. "I know it's good to tell an adult when you're having problems, but . . . I don't know. I think it's better for me to do this on my own."

"Well, it's important to stand up for yourself," Kat said slowly. She knew from first-hand experience how hard that could be.

The girls left the schoolyard and headed down the street. "Maybe Megan's just not very self-confident and she's mean to me to make herself feel better," said Grace.

Kat was impressed. "Maybe," she said.

"In any case, don't worry," said Grace. "I'm sure I'll be able to work it out. Somehow."

"Okay. Just let me know if I can help." Kat grinned. "But in the meantime, the puppies are waiting."

"And the interview will start soon!" added Grace.

Kat pulled Grace's arm. "Come on, slow poke! Let's run. Last one to Tails Up is a rotten tomato!"

CHAPTER NINE

"Here he is. Kat, Grace, meet Bill Bracer. He's come to speak with us about our bichon frise puppies," said Aunt Jenn. She led the man into the doggy-daycare room.

"Hello, girls," said Bill Bracer. He had snow-white hair and a bushy white beard. His back was a little stooped, and he walked with a cane. He had a big smile. But when he saw the three puppies in the kennel, his smile grew even bigger. "Well, aren't they something!" he said.

Mr. Bracer went right over and looked in at the puppies. He put his fingers through one of the openings. Aimée and Chantal wiggled and wagged. They poked their little noses at him. Bijou sat to the side and watched, curious.

"Would you like to hold one of the puppies?" Aunt Jenn asked. She nodded to Kat.

"This one is a girl. Her name is Chantal," Kat told Mr. Bracer, pointing. "This is Chantal's sister. Her name is Aimée." Then she pointed toward Bijou. "And this is Bijou, the only boy."

Kat watched closely. Mr. Bracer smiled, but he didn't even seem to look at Bijou.

"Bijou is quiet but he's sweet," Kat added quickly. She couldn't help it.

"Well, I'm sure he is, but I do so like the look of this little pup here," Mr. Bracer said, pointing to Aimée. "Seems awfully friendly. Could I please hold her?"

Aunt Jenn nodded. Kat picked up Aimée and handed her to Mr. Bracer. He hung his cane on his arm and took the puppy carefully, pulling her close to his chest.

"Oh, my. You are lovely, Aimée," he said. "A sweet little handful of fluff!" Mr. Bracer looked into the kennel again. "That other little brown-eyed gal looks very sweet as well," he said. "May I hold her, too?"

Kat looked at Aunt Jenn, who nodded. She

picked up Chantal and handed her to Mr. Bracer.

Kat grinned as the puppies wiggled happily, licking each other's faces.

"These sisters are good pals," said Mr. Bracer jovially. "They remind me of my last pair of dogs. They were sisters, too. Pugs. One never went anywhere without the other! Well, Aimée and Chantal, wouldn't it be nice if I could take you both home with me?"

Grace nudged Kat and lifted her eyebrows. "Both puppies?" she whispered. "He wants both!"

Kat nodded, excited. "Wouldn't that be great?" she whispered back.

Aunt Jenn cleared her throat. "So, Mr. Bracer," she said, her voice solemn. "You've answered all my questions already, but Grace and Kat have a few more questions they'd like to ask you, if that's all right."

"Oh, my, my, yes. I bet they have something

to do with what it said on the poster, correct?"
Mr. Bracer said.

He looked at Kat and Grace. "So here are
your answers, girls. I memorized all the points.
They were that important to me." He winked
at them. "Kind and loving? You bet. Willing to
go on walks? Rain or snow? Indeedy. Need a
very special friend? I should say so." He hugged
Aimée and Chantal close. "You can count on me
being a fine owner to these little gals. I'll treat
them like princesses. I promise."

Kat couldn't help but think about Bijou. "Mr.
Bracer, wouldn't you like to take Bijou as well?
The girls might be lonely without their brother,
and Bijou . . . well, he's quiet but he'll grow on
you, I know it!" she said.

The white-haired man shook his head. "If I
didn't have this cane, I might consider it, young
lady," he said, gently. "But I think these two are
really all I can handle."

Kat, Grace and Aunt Jenn had a quick, private meeting. All of them agreed that Mr. Bracer would be a wonderful owner for Aimée and Chantal.

Aunt Jenn handed Mr. Bracer a list of puppy instructions and a kit of doggy items that she had prepared. Tony helped carry the two puppies out to Mr. Bracer's car.

"I will certainly bring these gals back to visit you kind folks," Mr. Bracer said. "That's a promise, too."

Kat smiled back at him. She was sorry Bijou wasn't going along. But this was certainly a perfect match. Aimée and Chantal were in good hands.

After Mr. Bracer left, Kat and Grace played with Bijou together. They sat on the floor across from each other and rolled a ball between them. Bijou ran back and forth, chasing the ball. Kat and Grace laughed as the little puppy tried to pick up the ball.

"It's too big," Kat told him. "And your mouth is just too small!"

After a while, Grace sighed. "I have to go home early," she said. "I promised my mom I'd work on my math homework before dinner."

She said goodbye to Bijou and Kat.

Kat was a little bit pleased. She liked having some time alone with Bijou. She picked up the puppy and cuddled him. She played tug-of-war with him. She practised "sit" with him, giving him a little piece of dog biscuit when he followed her command.

She felt sad putting him back in the empty kennel. "Will you miss your sisters?" she asked.

But Bijou didn't look unhappy. He curled up in a corner of the kennel, wagged his tail twice, and then closed his eyes.

For a while Kat just stood and looked at him.

She worried Bijou might not win anyone's heart but hers. Today, for example, Mr. Bracer had poked his fingers in the crate and said hello to the puppies. But Bijou hadn't come over like his sisters had.

Of course, not all puppies were the same. Just like people.

Kat thought about Maya. She was like Aimée and Chantal — enthusiastic and eager from the get-go. Grace was more like Bijou — neither of them jumped into things. It didn't mean they didn't like to have fun. It didn't mean they weren't friendly. They just took their time to show it.

"Bye, Bijou," Kat whispered to the sleeping pup. "I really hope someone will show up here who will love you as much as I do!"

CHAPTER TEN

On Wednesday and again on Thursday, Kat, Grace and Maya went to Tails Up after school. They played ball with Bijou. Kat spent more time teaching him to sit on command.

Each day Aunt Jenn told them that several people had called about the abandoned bichon frise puppies, but none of them were the best fit for Bijou.

Kat was getting more and more worried.

But when Kat, Maya and Grace arrived at Tails Up on Friday, Aunt Jenn had a smile on her face. "Good news! A family is coming this afternoon to see Bijou," she told them. "Let's keep our fingers crossed that this is a good match! I'll bring them into the doggy-daycare room when they arrive."

"Oh, phew!" breathed Maya with relief. She slapped her hand to her chest dramatically. "Now Bijou's self-esteem won't be shattered for all time!"

"Maya!" protested Kat. But she couldn't stop grinning.

A family was coming to see Bijou! A family who had passed Aunt Jenn's phone inspection. This was the puppy's big chance!

The girls went into the doggy-daycare room. Kat went to the kennel. When Bijou saw her, he wagged his tail. But he stayed sitting in the corner, as always.

"Oh, Bijou," Kat said, picking him up. "You are so calm and quiet. You are a very special puppy!"

"I hope the family coming today can see that!" Maya said.

Kat cuddled the puppy and then set him down. "This might be the last time we get to play with you," she told him. "So let's have fun!"

Grace dangled a knotted rope toy in front of Bijou, then she threw it across the room. "Here you go, Bijou! Go get it!"

The girls played with the puppy for about an hour. Kat felt happy and sad at the same time — happy that Bijou might get a new home, sad that she might not be able to see him again. She kept looking at the time. She kept waiting for the daycare room door to open.

Then finally it did.

"This is where we keep our boarders," Aunt Jenn was saying. "And this is where we are keeping Bijou right now."

Kat scooped up Bijou so he wouldn't try to run into the hallway. Then she turned to look at the new family. Her mouth dropped open. Then she frowned.

No. No way.

CHAPTER ELEVEN

Aunt Jenn smiled at the girls. "Kat, Grace, Maya, meet Mr. and Mrs. Fernandez and their daughter Megan."

"Hello," said Maya. "Nice to meet you."

Kat and Grace were too surprised to speak. Megan! It was Megan.

They stared at their classmate. Then they looked at each other. Megan squirmed uncomfortably.

Maya shot Kat a puzzled look, sensing something was going on.

"Do you girls know one another?" Aunt Jenn said, noticing the silence.

"We . . . we're in the same class," said Megan. She gave a little wave. "Hey, Kat. Grace."

Still the girls didn't speak. But Aunt Jenn continued on with her introductions. "And this," she said, pointing toward the puppy in Kat's arms, "is Bijou."

"Oh, he's so sweet," said Megan. She clasped her hands together. "Look at him, Mom and Dad. Isn't he sweet?"

"Yes, he sure is," agreed Megan's mother.

Megan's father smiled happily and nodded.

Megan came toward Kat, as if Bijou were a magnet. Her eyes were glued to the white bichon frise puppy.

"Hello there, Bijou," she said gently. "Oh, you're adorable!"

"Kat," said Aunt Jenn. "Can you let Megan hold him?"

Kat glared at Megan, but Megan didn't even notice. Kat wanted to say no. She wanted to tell Megan that she couldn't have Bijou, even for a moment.

"Kat?" Aunt Jenn repeated.

Grace nodded at her to follow Aunt Jenn's instructions.

Carefully, Kat handed the puppy to Megan.

Bijou went very still in Megan's arms. He didn't try to kiss her. He didn't wag his tail.

But Megan didn't seem to mind. She held Bijou nicely. She rubbed his ears, just the way he liked it. She kissed his little nose.

"He's perfect," said Megan, her voice trembling. "Just perfect."

Next Mr. and Mrs. Fernandez took turns holding Bijou. Then they set down the puppy. He ran to Kat and hid behind her legs.

"That's okay," said Megan to her parents. "He just needs to get used to us."

Megan sat on the floor near Kat. Quietly she held out her hand. "Here, Bijou," she called. "Come and say hello when you're ready."

Kat wanted to scoop Bijou up and hug him, but instead she waited to see what he would do. She had to give Megan a chance. For Bijou's sake. And in a few minutes, Bijou did go over to Megan. He sniffed her hand and then licked it. In a moment, he climbed right up into her lap and made himself comfortable.

Megan's parents were speaking to each other. Then Mr. Fernandez turned and said, "We would very much like to take Bijou home with us. We would like him to be our very own puppy, if it's all right with you."

Aunt Jenn smiled. "Very good," she said. "You've answered all my questions already on the phone. It's up to Grace, Maya and Kat now."

Megan looked down at Bijou. She stroked the puppy's head. She was clearly uncomfortable.

Kat wanted to ask, "How can we give you a puppy when we don't think you're a nice person? Will you stop teasing me about Owen? Will you stop teasing Grace, too?"

But she decided not to. Grace had told Kat that she wanted to work it out with Megan on her own. So Kat would leave it to Grace. This was her big chance. Now Megan could see how it felt when people were mean. Kat turned to Grace and nodded encouragingly.

Megan looked worried. She was biting her lip. She held Bijou close.

Grace fixed Megan in a stare. But all Grace said was, "Megan. Do you promise to be loving to Bijou? Do you promise to be kind?"

Megan kissed Bijou on the top of his little white head. She took a breath and looked right into Grace's eyes. Megan's voice shook a little. "Yes, I'll be loving. I'll be kind. I promise." She looked at Grace and Kat. "I know I'm not always the nicest person in the world. But I promise to be Bijou's very best friend. I will take very, very good care of him."

If Megan wasn't teasing everyone all the time, Kat thought, *I might even believe her. She sounds like she means it.*

For a long moment, Grace and Megan just looked at each other.

Kat waited. What was Grace going to say? This was her chance to make Megan sorry for the way she had treated her.

But Grace didn't say anything. And then Aunt Jenn was saying cheerfully, "All right then, Fernandez family. We'll just leave you for a moment with Bijou. Kat, Grace, Maya and I need to have a quick meeting. Then we'll tell you our decision."

Kat followed her two friends and Aunt Jenn into the hallway.

"So, what do you think, girls?" Aunt Jenn asked. She pumped her fist into the air once, twice. "Perfect, right?"

Maya nodded. "They get my vote," she said.

"I think they will give our sweet little Bijou a good home," agreed Aunt Jenn. "Kat? Grace? You two agree?"

Kat looked at Grace. But Grace was deep in thought.

"Grace?" Aunt Jenn asked.

Kat nudged Grace. "Go on," she whispered. "Tell her."

Grace shook her head.

"What is it?" Aunt Jenn asked. "Is there something I should know? Kat?"

Grace shook her head again at Kat, like a warning.

"No," Grace said quickly. "There's nothing. And yes." Suddenly she smiled. "Yes, I think Megan and her family will give Bijou a good home." She nodded. "And you do too, don't you, Kat?"

Kat stared at her friend. "You're sure?" she asked.

"Yup. I'm sure," Grace said firmly. Kat was surprised. But it was up to Grace. And even though Grace didn't always seem like the most self-confident girl in the world, Kat had confidence in her.

When they went back inside and told the Fernandez family the news, Kat saw Megan's face light up.

"Thank you," she said to Aunt Jenn and Maya.

Megan approached Kat and Grace. "Thank

you," she said to the two girls. "Very much." She hugged Bijou close. Her voice was shaky again. "I never thought I'd be able to have my own puppy, especially one as sweet as Bijou."

Kat sighed with relief. Bijou had a home and a best friend. And Megan actually seemed like she would take really good care of him.

Maybe this girl is different than she seems on the outside. Just like another girl I know, Kat thought, thinking of Grace. She grinned. *And just like a sweet little bichon frise puppy I know*, Kat thought, thinking, of course, of Bijou himself.

CHAPTER TWELVE

Maya, Grace and Kat sat on the floor of Kat's bedroom.

Grace was sticking photos of the bichon frise puppies into the Puppy Collection scrapbook. Kat was drawing a picture of them.

"How's this?" Maya stuck the pencil behind her ear and read aloud: "Chantal, Aimée and Bijou are bichon frises. They are two months old. Chantal and Aimée are sisters. They are lively and outgoing. They like to be together! Bijou is their brother. He likes to take his time getting to know people. He is quiet and very sweet."

"Nice," said Kat. "Just right."

"So, which of you is going to tell me what was going on this afternoon?" Maya asked. She raised her eyebrows.

Kat looked at Grace.

"Go ahead," Grace said, grinning.

So Kat told Maya the whole story. "That was *your* Megan?" Maya asked. "Megan from your class?" Maya's mouth dropped open as she listened. She knew Megan had been mean to Kat but she didn't know Megan had been mean to Grace, too.

"She's so annoying," said Maya, shaking her head. "I can't believe you both agreed to give her Bijou! You could have told Jenn that Megan was mean. She'd never have given Bijou to her."

Grace grinned. "Yeah, I know," she agreed. "But I thought we should give her a chance. Not just judge her because of the way she is to us. She was able to see right through to the sweetness inside Bijou. I thought we should try to do the same for her. I have a feeling she'll be wonderful with this puppy."

"Maybe," Maya said, slowly. "Maybe you're right."

But Kat said, firmly, "Well, I know you are. Good call, Grace."

Grace began to blush. So Kat quickly said, "And now, you lucky, lucky friends, I have a special treat for you." Her eyes twinkled. "Not only are you invited to have dinner with me tonight, but you also get one more joke for today!"

Maya rolled her eyes. "Oh no!"

Grace laughed. "Really. It's not necessary," she protested.

"It is absolutely no problem. I know how

much you both like these," Kat insisted. "Here goes: What kind of dog loves to take bubble baths?"

"No. No," Maya said, groaning. "I refuse to listen." She slapped her hands over her ears.

Grace giggled.

Kat tried to look offended. It was difficult when her mouth kept wanting to smile.

"Okay, okay, put us out of our misery," said Maya. "What kind of dog loves to take bubble baths?"

"Why, a shampoodle, of course!" announced Kat.

"So, so bad!" moaned Maya.

"So, so, so bad!" groaned Grace.

For more puppy fun, check out these other books!

Piper's First Show

ISBN 978-1-4431-3360-9

Kat and her friends help Aunt Jenn train a puppy, a four-month-old Bernese mountain dog named Piper, for her first puppy show. They only need to work on a few simple commands, but the girls soon find out that training a puppy is not as easy as it seems . . . Can the girls get Piper ready for the show in time?

Cricket's Close Call

ISBN 978-1-4431-3362-3

Kat, Maya and Grace are on puppy duty once more. This time they're helping Aunt Jenn look after a Yorkshire terrier puppy named Cricket. Cricket is tiny but he's full of energy. He has a habit of trying to eat anything he comes across. The girls have to do their best to keep him out of trouble.

Houdini's Escape

ISBN 978-1-4431-4650-0

When a beagle named Houdini comes to board at Tails Up, he turns out to be a master escape artist. Kat, Maya and Grace foil two of his escape attempts, but it's not long before Houdini manages to sneak away from under their noses. Will the girls be able to find the missing puppy?

Nutmeg All Alone

ISBN 978-1-4431-4652-4

When a tiny Cavalier King Charles spaniel comes to board at Tails Up, Aunt Jenn calls on Kat, Maya and Grace to help look after her. But Nutmeg isn't like any puppy they've met before. She seems so sad most of the time. And when she stops eating altogether, the girls become quite worried. Will they be able to cheer up this sad, lonely puppy?